MEGAN J. PARKER
Scarlet Dawn

Copyright © 2014 by Megan J. Parker
Edited by Nathan Squiers for Tiger Dynasty Publishing
Cover art by ShinyShadows (DeviantArt)
FRONT Formatting Art by Samantha Jenkins
Design by Eden Crane Designs
ISBN-13: 978-1-940634-14-2

This is a work of fiction. Names, characters places, and incidents either are the product of the author's imagination or are used fictitiously. Any resemblance to actual persons living or dead, events, or locales is entirely coincidental.

If you purchased this book without a cover you should be aware that this book is stolen property. It was reported as "unsold and destroyed" to the publisher and neither the author nor the publisher has received any payment for this "stripped book."

All rights reserved. No part of this book may be reproduced or transmitted in any form or by any means, electronic or mechanical, including photocopying, recording, or by any information storage and retrieval system, without the written permission of the Publisher, except where permitted by law.

Grace,
Thanks for stopping by!

Dedicated to all those who believe in the transcendence of love past the flesh and through the spirit.

ACKNOWLEDGEMENTS

I would like to thank EVERYONE who has stood by me since the first publication (and several re-releases) of Scarlet Night. While time progressed, I really appreciated the patience and dedication you all put forth for me!

Also, a special thanks to my fiancé and fellow author, Nathan Squiers, for not only editing this bad boy but contributing to the backstory in "There and Back Again" as well as the dream chapter, "Lullaby of the Crucified" and "Closing In". This sequel would not be the same without you!!

This sequel is *long* past due (and, believe me, I appreciate the absence of ANY bomb mail appearing at my doorstep *deep breath*)…

So, while I could sit here and spout all sorts of thanks to everyone who had a part in making this sequel come to fruition, let's get to the good shit!

THANK YOU & I HOPE YOU ENJOY! Xoxo

Your one & only Scarlet Empress,

Megan J. Parker

"LOVE IS A SMOKE RAISED WITH THE FUME OF SIGHS"
- WILLIAM SHAKESPEARE

PROLOGUE

"I DON'T KNOW HOW TO EXPLAIN IT. I just *know* that Zane is still out there somewhere." Serena sighed and choked down the newest batch of synthetic blood, "Oh! Blech! Ahg! Sweet shit, Zoey! What'd you put in this one? Badger piss?"

"Quit complaining and drink it," Zoey sighed, not looking away from the file on their newest mission from The Council. "And I'm not questioning your instincts," she retrieved the pen she'd tucked behind her ear, causing a wave of blue-dyed hair to fan across her face, "A part of me wants to believe that he's still alive, too. But you're letting it get in the way of what needs to be done."

"What needs to be done? Really?" Serena rolled her eyes and pulled the file away, "*This* is nothing more than another distraction! They're just trying to swamp us with new assignments because they think I'm—"

"Dangerously obsessed?" Zoey frowned, finally looking up at her.

Serena growled and threw the file back on the table. "Dammit, Zoey, not you too!"

The corners of Zoey's eyes dropped as a wave of sympathy rolled off of her aura—the rippling energy signature matching her hair—and she wetted her lips before letting them part to—

"No!" Serena aimed a stern index finger at her, "You *will not* do this to me. Not now! You *know* what they're doing; keeping me busy just so I don't..." She bit her lip, "Just so I don't..."

Zoey stepped over and wrapped her arms around her friend, "Just so you don't do this to yourself." She nodded, "And I thank them for that every day."

Ever since getting her power-hungry brother, Keith, arrested by The Council, the non-human government had recognized Serena as capable of handling the role of leader of her late-father's clan. And while the respect was a refreshing change of pace, an unwelcome reunion with a bitch-vamp named Kristine from her past shortly after had taken her lover's life and turned their victory into a bitter-sweet mess. However, never one to make *anything* simple, Zane's "death" had only seemed to take his aura—his *being*—out of the picture and allowed for his old friend, Raith, to take control of his body; a bizarre turn of events that now forced Serena to *see* Zane on a daily basis while still being expected to believe that he was gone.

And the whole ordeal was most certainly taking its toll.

Though she would never admit it to Zoey—not that it mattered, since the auric vampire's psychic abilities could spot that little detail easily—Serena *was* suffering, and The Council's distractions *were* probably the only thing keeping her sane.

Still...

She shivered as she imagined Zane's mismatched, silver-and-blue gaze and the flash of that devious grin of his that always made her toes curl. And the way his fingers...

"Earth to Serena," Zoey called as she waved her hand in front of Serena's face. "Hey, airhead, you in there?"

"Yeah," Serena nodded, "Sorry, just got lost in thought."

"About what?" Zoey frowned.

Knowing that the subject of Zane would only result in more nauseating pity and even more lectures, Serena put up a psychic shield to hide her thoughts and forced a wicked grin that she'd all-but trained herself to wear by that point. "This delicious hunk of yes-ness I saw in the latest Vogue. He was a hottie-hot-hottie!" Serena winked to sell the lie, "Oh, Zoey, the things I would do…"

"That's fine! I trust you, Serena! I don't need to hear about the things you'd do. I'm still not fully recovered from that cayenne pepper scenario you chose to share," Zoey chuckled as she moved the file back towards Serena, "Now, are you ready to get some work done?"

Serena fought the urge to bite her lip and nodded, "Hell yea!"

Zoey smiled and pointed to the intel on the page. "Here's what The Council has so far on the rogue outlaw."

Serena sighed, studying the page and taking in the grainy, black-and-white picture that a poorly positioned security camera had captured.

"This?" Serena shook her head at the picture, "*This* stooge is the rogue that's eluded capture for so long? He's just a therion! Bait a damn bear trap with a Milk Bone and—oh… sorry, Zoey."

Her friend's aura whipped about in irritation as she shot a glare up at her.

"I take it back, okay? Therions… they have their charm," Serena offered an apologetic tug on Zoey's shoulder. "After all, Isaac couldn't have scored a babe like you if he wasn't a gentleman, right? Though I *have* heard that—"

Zoey cleared her throat, "The mission, Serena!"

"Oh, right," Serena giggled, nudging her friend once more before scanning over the file again. "Axle Travers: last seen… huh," Serena looked over her shoulder at a large map of the city they'd tacked to the wall, "That's only two hours from here. Why did we JUST get this file now? These cases are dated from several months ago!"

"Yeah, I guess he'd been quiet lately." Zoey shrugged, flipping through the pages before finally pulling a few of the last pages free and holding them up, "At least until recently."

"Okay, so what did this big, bad boy do recently to get The Council's panties in a bunch after such a long time of 'who gives a shit'?" Serena frowned.

Zoey shrugged, "Near as I can tell: he moved."

Serena frowned, "Huh?"

Zoey nodded, "No new charges. Just some intel on a shift in

whereabouts. See: an informant spotted him in our district about a week ago."

"Doing what?" Serena quirked an eyebrow.

"Uhm..." Zoey ran her fingertip over the report for a moment, "Buying a half-gallon of milk, I guess." She shrugged, "It doesn't look like he's done anything suspicious, but The Council seems convinced that, because of his history, he might be up to something."

Serena looked back at the picture, "So they want us to keep an eye on the stray dog just because he has a history of biting?"

Zoey sighed, "Though I'm not thrilled with your choice of metaphors, that *would* appear to be the case. However, there *has* been a rise in robberies and a few cases of arson since he was reported to have arrived, but The Council isn't interested in the affairs of the humans' laws."

"So even if he *is* the one responsible, The Council won't give two wet shits about it?" Serena frowned, "Doesn't a thieving therion register even as a blip on their radar?"

Zoey shook her head, "Not with what I've heard. Apparently they've got their hands full with a bunch of bodies that have been popping up with that Stryker-kid's name on them. *Literally!*"

"Mmm! That boy *is* a little cutey, though," Serena chuckled, "Wouldn't mind showing him a thing-or—"

"Really, Serena? *Really?* Is sex the *only* thing you think about?" Zoey shook her head, motioning back to the file. "Can we get back to the point? Remember: thieving therion?"

"Oh, right. Him..." Serena smirked, "Well then, I can only hope that he decides that good behavior isn't all it's cracked up to be."

"You *want* him to bring trouble into our area?" Zoey frowned up at her.

Serena nodded, "You bet! If this little crotch-sniffer stirs up more trouble, then The Council's gonna want results! I give them the results—bring in this unobtainable rogue—and they'll see that I'm not the nutcase that *everyone*"—she shot a look at Zoey—"seems to think I am. Then maybe they'll give me the support I need to finally track down that bitch Kristine and—"

"And continue this man-hunt for Zane?" Zoey turned to face her. "And what if he *is* gone, Serena; really, *really* gone!"

Serena growled, "Then I'll rip that murdering bitch apart!"

"What makes you so sure she's even still even alive?" Zoey frowned, "You and Raith... well, you weren't merciful."

"Yea, but the stupid cunt slipped away before we could finish the job," Serena growled, "And she made damn sure to mask her aura *and* her trail when she did. She might be a scabby twat-rag, but she's clever enough to stay hidden and stubborn enough to *not* die."

"Well if it makes any difference to you, I think Raith shares your sentiments. He wasn't at all pleased with her escape, either," Zoey shrugged. "Whether or not he got control of the body from it, he *was* Zane's friend. I'm sure he's every bit as furious at Kristine for attacking him. At least the *Maledictus* hasn't been active since he's taken control."

Serena bit her lip, "Any idea why that might be? Or why he was even in Zane's body in the first place?"

Zoey shook her head, "It all seems to have something to do with the curse that was put on Zane, but any memories that Raith might have aren't presenting themselves."

"Have you *actually* looked?" Serena looked over, "I mean *truly* tried to probe Raith's mind?"

Zoey frowned, "You can't ask me to invade somebody's privacy to that extent, Serena. I've only scanned him deep enough to know that he doesn't mean us any harm." She blushed and looked away, "And that his feelings for Nikki *are* sincere."

"Him and Nikki..." Serena sneered, shuddering at the memory of seeing Zane's body—freshly "possessed" by his old friend—locked in an embrace with their taroe comrade and...

"I know. I wasn't expecting that either," Zoey sighed.

Serena clenched her fists, "Maybe if those two would quit being lovey-dovey long enough to explain *anything* then we might find Zane."

Zoey bit her lip, "And then maybe you'll stop putting holes in your bedroom walls every time they're together?"

Serena felt her fangs begin to extend and she growled, "If I find out they're bumping nasties I'm gonna—"

"Serena!" Zoey took her wrist in her left hand and Serena felt the flood of anger begin to numb, "Whether you like it or not you need to remember that *that* isn't Zane."

"It's..." Serena struggled to keep her thoughts focused even as Zoey's auric efforts calmed her boiling mind, "It's still... his body."

Zoey nodded, "And we'll deal with the situation when the time comes, but in the meantime..." She slowly withdrew her hand when she saw that Serena's mind was calm.

Serena offered a thankful nod. "In the meantime, we keep ourselves busy," she looked back down at the papers, grinning at the picture of Axle; their newest assignment. Her newest distraction. "What do you say we go find this Axle guy and see if we can't stir up some fun?"

Zoey smiled and nodded, "I love that idea... but can I ask for one little, itsy-bitsy favor?"

"What's up, Zoe?" Serena grinned, already beginning to pull on her steel-toed boots.

Zoey blushed, "Can I drive?"

CHAPTER ONE
THE CHASE

"OH GOD... OH GOD... OH GO—Why did I let you talk me into letting YOU drive again?" Zoey cried out as Serena downshifted into a squealing drift that carried the green convertible across two lanes of oncoming traffic. Halfway through the turn, Serena threw the clutch and floored the gas pedal, sending them rocketing forward between an eighteen-wheeler and a honking Jeep before she jerked the wheel and returned the car to the right side of the road. "Dear Jesus! Blessed Buddha! Humble Shiva! Sweet Satan... SOMEBODY—ANYBODY—SAVE ME!!"

"Because you KNOW you actually have fun with me driving! Come on, Zoey! Let loose for once!" Serena laughed as she quickly moved to the right land and swerved across two lanes onto their exit.

"C-can't you slow down just a litt—AH SHIT!" Zoey cried, grabbing hold of edge of the windshield and whimpering, "Why did you have to get a convertible?"

Serena smirked, "Because it's fun to see you flail without an 'oh shit' handle to grab hold of! Too bad Isaac's not here; I hear he's got quite an 'oh shit' ha—"

Zoey's eyes widened, "KEEP YOUR EYES ON THE ROAD!"

Serena swerved around the oncoming car and slipped back into her lane without taking her eyes off her friend, "You're too tense, you know that, right?"

Making it into the more populated area of the city, Serena slowed the car and began to look around the streets.

"You said they'd be in this area, Zoey. Where do I turn now?" She scanned the sleepy business district, the towering buildings—dark and vacant—providing no sign of *any* sort of activity; mythos or otherwise. Sighing, Serena turned onto another street.

"Wait! Did you hear that?" Zoey frowned.

Focusing her superhuman ears, Serena picked up on the squeal of an alarm in the distance and she smirked, "Good ear, Zoe!"

Zoey bit her lip, "Does this mean…?"

"Oh you *know* it, sister!" Serena howled excitedly as she hit the gas and spun in the direction of the sound.

Zoey cried out as Serena weaved in and out of the lighter traffic filled areas. Zoey screamed as they sailed through two red lights and nearly collided with a pickup truck.

"What a rush!" Serena smirked, turning the wheel as they made it to the source and she slammed the brakes. The convertible's tires shrieked louder than the alarm as it came to an abrupt stop and Serena threw it in park before vaulting over the door and turning to wait on her friend.

Zoey, still dizzy and disoriented from the ride, slowly opened her side and stepped out of the car on shaky legs. "Go get 'em, Serena," she waved her friend on as she began to catch her breath, leaning on the car for support, "I'm… uh, I'm right behind ya… oh god, I think I'm gonna puke."

Serena smirked and nodded, sprinting through the open door and into the dark interior of the building. Seeing no immediate cause of the alarms, she cast out her aura and began to scan the rooms for any sign of the intruders.

"Looking for someone, toots?" A voice called from behind and the sound of heavy footsteps followed.

"Yea, some friends of mine were worried about a stray dog that's been wandering about," Serena turned and glared, recognizing Axle Travers from the photo in his file. As far as dirty rogues went, he *was* surprisingly handsome; a definite step-up from the eyesore mythos lawbreakers Serena usually had to deal with. With a pair of gleeful, animalistic green eyes that gazed out from under a mat of shaggy, dirty-blond hair all atop a face that was deliciously boyish-yet-chiseled, he certainly was in a league of his own. He wore nothing but a greasy tank-top that might have passed for white at one time and a baggy pair of even more greasy jeans. She frowned, realizing she was staring for a moment and—extending a half-hearted appreciation for Zoey's accusation of her sex-starved mind—forced herself to look away from his features and down at his hand.

"So what's in the bag?" Serena frowned, "More greasy laundry? On your way to the laundromat?"

"We were," Axle smirked and shrugged, "but then we remembered that we'd left our quarters at home and we didn't have any bills to break. So... well, you know how it is."

Serena sneered, "Stealing money? Really? What would you need money for anyway?"

Axle pouted, "You don't believe my laundry story?"

"Did you really expect me to?" Serena pursed her lips.

"Hmm... I guess not," he shrugged. "Fair enough, I suppose." He paused to take her in, his eyes lighting up as he made no effort to hide his ogling, "Though I might be persuaded to be a little more... umm, cooperative..." He stepped forward giving her a teasing wink.

"How's this for persuasion?" Serena jumped forward, slamming her booted foot into his stomach.

He growled and stumbled back before catching himself and narrowing his eyes. "You broke my smolder!" He grinned slightly, however his eyes still held the pain he was in from her kick.

"Yea, I guess this is kinda an off-day for you. Now, I'm going to relieve you of that heavy burden, and then I'm gonna bring you in for The Council to deal with," she grinned, stepping forward and going to reach for the bag of money.

Axle frowned, "The Council?" He sneered, stepping back, "*You're* a clan warrior?"

"Don't sound so surprised, ass-hat!" Serena glared, "And I'll have you know I'm a clan *leader!*"

"Oh…" He sized her up again, "Slim pickins for your kin, I see. My condolences."

As Serena lunged for the bag, he yanked it away and swiped his leg out, taking her legs out from under her and sending her flat on her ass, glaring up at him.

"I think I'm going to like this city a lot more than I thought," Axle smirked and turned away, starting towards five hooded figures who appeared behind him; each one toting their own bag of stolen loot.

"You are going to pay for that!" Serena called out after him, jumping back to her feet.

"I've got the cops driving in circles two blocks east of here, boss," one of the hooded figures—an auric from what Serena could see—called out to him, handing him his bags. As the others also forfeited their cargo to their leader, they all looked back towards Serena, "You want us to deal with that?"

Axle shook his head, "No. I think I'd like to see her again in a future adventure." Glancing back, the therion winked at her, "Until then, doll."

"Doll?" Serena started towards them, "You little—" An auric blast caught her off guard and sent her sprawling back. By the time her head stopped spinning and her eyes regained focus, she saw the last of the rogues jumping out the window. "God dammit!"

Sprinting after them, Serena launched herself through the window and, still airborne, caught sight of Axle and his gang driving through the streets towards the highway. Below her, Zoey was already pulling the car around.

"At'ta girl, Zoey!" Serena smiled and threw out her purple aura, securing a hold on the car and pulling herself into the driver's seat right as Zoey slipped back into the passenger side. "You feeling better?"

Zoey rolled her eyes, "Does it make a difference? Just get after them!"

"Don't gotta tell my ass twice!" Serena pushed in the clutch and slammed her foot on the gas as she threw the car into gear. The sound of gears violently meeting echoed into the night and the sudden lurch caused Zoey to let out a breathy squeal as they peeled off after the rogues' car. "Couple of pussies in a pussy-ass Jag ain't getting' away from me!" She grinned as she sped after them.

Zoey frowned, "Isn't this a Jaguar too? What's the difference?"

Serena rolled her eyes, "Theirs is *red*! Don't you know *anything* about cars?"

"Not entirely confident that you do..." Zoey bit her lip.

"It's really quite simple," Serena started. "You see— motherfuckers!"

As they began to catch up, Axle made a sharp left onto a side street, forcing Serena to interrupt her speech and quickly jerk the wheel to keep on them, their car fishtailing and nearly spinning them out into the sidewalk.

"Serena! You're going to get us killed!" Zoey cried out as she hunched forward, looking sick to her stomach.

"Asshole's grandmother must've taught him how to drive!" Serena growled as she righted the car and began to chase them down once more. The chase worked its way from Main Street onto a highway onramp, where the two wove around several slower moving cars.

As the two cars roared down the nearly-empty interstate, Serena began to close in on them. She watched as Axle, motioning to one of his gang members, sacrificed the driver's seat and jumped onto the trunk of his car.

Zoey frowned, "What is he...?"

As the two watched, the hand Axle was using to stabilize himself shifted and transformed into a muscular and clawed therion hand. Digging his fingertips into the car and securing himself, Axle smirked and used his free hand to casually wave at Serena.

"HEY, DOLL! WASN'T EXPECTING TO SEE YOU SO SOON!"

"That pretentious... the fucking nerve!" Serena growled as she shifted gears and floored the accelerator, bringing the chase to over 100mph.

"Serena! You're going to overheat the engine!" Zoey cried out.

"He is not getting away, Zoey!" Serena smirked, wrapping her bright purple aura around the car and the car began to lift off of the street.

Noticing this, Axle called back to his gang. A moment later, an orange aura surrounded their car as well.

"You cheap bastard," Serena shook her head. "Zoey! I need you to slow them down!"

Zoey nodded and Serena watched as a bright blue auric tendril reached out from her chest and began to strike at the orange aura that was carrying the gang's car.

"That's it, Zoey! We've got him now!" Serena smirked.

In a clash of blue and orange, Zoey's jabs at the orange aura caused it to lower the car to the street so that it could lash back at her attacks. Unable to see auras and, therefore, oblivious of the scene around him, Axle glanced back at his crew as his car began to slow down. Serena grinned at Axle's confused look as she pushed with her own aura to move their own car closer.

"That's right, you son of a bitch! We've got *two* aurics, and you've only got—oh, come on!" Before she could finish, Serena spotted a green bolt extend from one of the other members of Axle's gang and snake its way back, joining his comrade in fighting off Zoey's efforts.

"Serena! I don't know how much longer I can hold them off!! Their auras combined are too much!" Zoey cried out.

"Shit! I know, Zoey! Just hold on a little bit longer! We've almost made it up to them!!" Serena called out as she forced the car to gain even more speed with her auric hold.

"SERENA!"

Zoey's warning came too late as Axle hurled himself from the trunk of his car, his body exploding into his full therion form before landing on the hood of their own. Though he'd transformed in his more bestial form, Axle had retained the soft-yet-muscular features and dirty-blond hair.

"I thought they shot Ol' Yeller," Serena growled between clenched teeth, using her aura to rock the car in an attempt to shake their unwanted company.

Axle stumbled, but once again used his metal-piercing claws to secure himself to the car's siding and went to work ripping a hole in the hood.

Zoey whimpered, trying to keep her strength as she pushed back another attack. "Serena, I can't keep this up much—"

"I know!" Serena growled, trying to see past the hulking beast to the car ahead of them, "Just a bit longer, Zoe! Please, you can do this!"

Axle drove his clawed hand into the depths of the car and Serena heard the engine begin to sputter as he began ripping the guts from under the hood.

"What are you doing to my baby, you fucker?" Serena glared, wishing she could strike out with her aura but knowing she'd be dropping their car onto the unforgiving street at over 200mph if she released a portion of her hold on it.

Tossing a few of his prizes over the side of the car, Axle began to transform back into his human form. "It's nothing personal, toots," he offered when his face and vocal cords were back to normal, "but you *are* cramping my style. Call me sometime, though."

Serena glared, "You ass-sniffing mong—HEY!"

But Axle had already leapt back to the trunk of his car, securing himself in place at the driver's seat once again.

"Ser-en-a!" Zoey's voice cracked with each syllable as she fought to hold the aurics' forces back. As her hold on the battle wavered, her aura shifted and broke—withdrawing back into her chest—and the two aurics, now free to reach the car, seized Serena's own and broke her hold on the car.

As the tires made contact with the street, they began to feel their gained momentum lag as they slowed down. Slamming her foot repeatedly on the gas but finding no reaction from doing so, Serena began cursing as the now-smoking car stuttered and began to skid out of control off the road and into the Nevada desert.

"Bastards! Those fucking bastards!" She ground out between clenched teeth, slamming her fist against the steering wheel with each word, bending it inward until it finally was torn free from the dashboard.

"Serena..." Zoey said flatly, not taking her eyes from the night-bathed desert ahead of her.

"Don't say it, Zoey. Don't you dare even—"

"Next time, I drive!" She grumbled, ignoring Serena's growls as she pitched her head over the door and finally threw up.

CHAPTER TWO
THE BEAUTIFUL PEOPLE

AXLE SMIRKED, WATCHING IN HIS rearview mirror as his pursuers disappeared in the distance.

"Man! That was close!" Axle smirked. "Well done, boys! You really did me proud back there! I was *almost* afraid she'd get us."

"As if! She was not even close to getting us!" Tristan grinned, "Though it *was* the first time I've ever had to lift an entire car just to avoid being caught. Wouldn't mind doing *that* again!"

"None of that was supposed to be fun!" Drake growled, turning to glare at the other three in the back.

Frowning, Axle stayed quiet as he took an exit off the highway and started up the road towards the gutted factory.

"That was too close for my liking," Drake went on, "And if we intend to stay here and do what we're doing, we have to do this right." He narrowed his eyes at Tristan, "If Lucas hadn't jumped in with his aura when he did, then that blue-haired bitch would've smeared us all over the pavement... and I think we all know that snarky dyke would've finished whichever of us weren't already dead!"

"Oh come on, Drake! We made it, didn't we? We got the money *and* we got to stick it to the local law!" Shayne paused and shrugged, smirking, "Though the one with blue hair *was* kind of cute! Had a sort of Sailor Moon vibe to her."

Quinn frowned and shook his head, his sangsuigan fangs extended in response to his irritation. "No! Drake's right! We're not here to have fun and play Cops and Robbers with the local clan! We have a job to do and this stunt nearly fucked it up!"

Axle frowned and shook his head, "Drake! Quinn! Chill-ax! We got the job done, but if either of you thought that we'd dodge the officials forever then you were *both* fooling yourselves! Everyone did *exactly* what needed to be done back there, and, in case you haven't noticed, we're *here*! Nobody's dead and the money is where it needs to be!" He looked over at Drake, his childhood friend, whose body was so tense that it was noticeably beginning to shift into his therion form. Resting a hand on his shoulder, he sighed "Don't worry so much. You drove like a beast back there, man! How could you think we'd *not* come out of this alright when you've got moves like that? And you"—he looked over at Quinn—"you made some great calls back there! I hadn't even realized what those vamp-chicks were doing before you made the call to Tristan to take us off the road... *literally!*" He nodded to them, "You guys did great, but don't take out your tension on the others; they're just letting off a little tension after our big encounter. Either way, I can handle them."

Sighing, Drake nodded and allowed his body settling back in its human form.

As they pulled up to the old factory, the tension began to subside. After Axle parked in the cracked and dusty parking lot near the long-unused loading area, he nodded to the others to collect the bags and glanced over at Lucas, who bit his lip as he felt a pair of eyes on him.

Offering the shy auric a reassuring smile, Axle nodded, "You really saved our butts back there."

"Th-thanks," Lucas' shoulders eased noticeably in reaction to the compliment.

Axle gave him a pat on the shoulder, "Keep an eye out for

anything while we get the bags inside, okay?"

Lucas nodded and stepped out with the others, leaning against the car and closing his eyes to let his aura do what it did best, nodding to him when he was certain that there were no unwanted onlookers.

As the group brought the bags inside, they were greeted by the many excited cries of children, who rushed towards them to celebrate their return.

"Oh no! They're gonna get us!" Quinn play-cried as he saw the wave of young mythos orphans, and he quickly let go the two bags he was carrying and dropped to his knees to play-wrestle with the kids that honed on him in a group tackle.

Axle smiled, seeing Quinn laugh and play. Though it was hard to get him to operate on any setting but "serious" anywhere else, the moment he was around the kids the fun-loving side emerged. This, however, came as little surprise to any of the crew, who knew of Quinn's own history of growing up in such a setting. When he'd turned eighteen he decided to join Axle and the others to help raise more funds to keep the orphanage afloat. Though he was the youngest in their group, what he lacked in age he more than made up for in dedication. It was this dedication that had driven him to train and become one of the strongest sangs—young or old—that Axle had ever known.

"Man, I hope this all works out for them," Lucas stepped beside Axle. "Do you think that someday these kids can have a better place to stay? This isn't fair for them."

Drake frowned and shook his head, "All that money and access to resources and The Council can't help?"

Axle shrugged, "Their parents lived as rogues—unregistered and denouncing any system—so, as far as The Council's records go, they don't exist." He looked back and sighed, "It's sad, yes, but The Council can't do anything about the things that so many have gone to such great lengths to keep them blind of. It will get better for them soon enough, though. I promise," Axle frowned as hefted three of the bags and headed further inside.

Getting to the top of a flight of stairs, he turned towards the gutted office, already hearing the muffled pitter-patter of tiny footsteps nearing behind him. Grinning, he pretended not to notice the sound until the source was nearly upon him, then...

"GOTCHA!" Dropping the bags, Axle turned in time to catch

the young vampire in mid-jump, "Oh, look at that! Your teeth are coming in nicely, Fang," he smiled, noticing that one of the young sang's fangs had grown longer than the other.

Fang was one of the newest additions to Sierra's orphanage, having been brought there a week earlier after Axle had first arrived. Though he'd been born to innocent, unregistered rogues, their lack of shelter had made them and their child easy targets for a group of mythos hunters. By the time Axle had come across the scene, Fang—who had expressed a preference in Axle's nickname for him over "Jace"—had already lost both of his parents and one his fangs. The humans were about to pull out the other, but had come to an untimely end at the end of Axle's claws.

"I know! I bit Elrik earlier to show him, but he didn't like that," Fang grinned.

"You bit Elrik?" Axle chuckled, "I'm sure Miss Sierra didn't like that, huh?"

"No, but Elrik liked it even less," Fang giggled and bounced in Axle's arms, "Are you going to stay longer today? I want to play!"

"I can't today, bud," Axle smiled softly, "but I promise next time I'll stay longer. We're just here now to drop off some things for Miss Sierra."

Fang pouted for a moment.

Behind Axle, the sound of high heels *clack*ing down the hall picked up as Sierra started towards them and Axle smirked, looking over his shoulder at her. She still had the same long, straight black hair and deep green eyes that she'd had when they were kids, but her years and assumed responsibilities had traded her once bouncy and casual demeanor with a stoic formality that only seemed to wane when Axle was able to rob a moment alone with her. It was his and Drake's childhood friendship with the sang vampire that had carried their investment in her efforts with rogue orphans as well as introducing them to the vampires of their gang. Because all of Sierra's initial efforts for the kids had been paid from her inheritance—an inheritance that had soon run out—the urgency for supplies had motivated the group to do all that they could to keep the hope alive...

Even if their methods *did* get him into trouble with The Council.

Setting Fang down and retrieving the bags, he held them up and smiled, "There's two more downstairs, I'd have brought them up, but Quinn was already drowning in kids and I think it's gonna take a full team to extract him *and* the bags he brought—OOPH!" He nearly toppled over as Sierra all-but threw herself around him in a tight and thankful embrace.

"Thank you so much, Axle! You really don't know how much this means to us!" She whimpered, snuggling her face into his chest, "I get so worried, though. I just wish there was another—"

"None of that," Axle felt his chest tighten and he softened his face as he pressed his palm to her tear-soaked cheek as he lifted her chin. "It'll be alright from now on. I promise," he smiled warmly and wiped a tear from her cheek, "No tears now, alright?"

She choked out a chuckle, nodding and quickly wiped her face and looked back to the bags and sighed, "I don't want to see you imprisoned by The Council. They can be ruthless!"

"As if they could catch us," Axle smirked. "I've been doing this every night for a week now and there are *zero* leads. *Nothing.* For the humans *and* The Council's lackeys." Though he wasn't happy about lying about the warriors they'd been lucky enough to escape from, he knew that telling her would do no good for either of them. Though Axle was proud of his therion roots, he often wished that he had the powers of an auric vampire—powers that would allow him to manipulate and shift emotions—to offer some aid to Sierra, who was prone to panic attacks. For a sang, she definitely didn't have the strength and confidence that ordinarily seemed the norm with her kind, and he constantly worried about her wellbeing given all the responsibilities she'd taken.

And what would happen to her and the kids if they were ever attacked…

As Axle started to pull his mind from the nerve-wracking thoughts, he heard the others starting up the steps behind him.

"Hey, Sierra," Tristan called out, "Did Axle tell you about the warriors that chased yet?"

Axle dropped his face into his palm.

"Chase?" Sierra's eyes went wide, "What kind of chase? Who was—"

"It's fine. Really! We just got chased by a few girls on the road," Axle smiled reassuringly.

"Psh! They weren't *just* girls!" Tristan beamed, "Clan warriors, Sierra! And we left them in the dust!"

Shayne smirked and nodded, "Oh man! Just *thinking* about that blue haired one is making my pants tighter! Oh god, the things I'd do!"

"Shut it! Both of you!" Axle glared as Sierra's cheeks turn bright pink. "You"—he pointed at Tristan—"learn to keep your mouth shut with pointless details. And you"—his finger shifted to Shayne—"the next time you talk like that in front of a lady I'm going to walk away with your *teeth* in my fist! Both of you got it?" The two nodded solemnly, "Good! Now take Fang and get out of here!"

As the two were escorted down the stairs by the young vampire, Axle fought the urge to laugh as he heard, "Wow! He really told you, huh? I bit Elrik today…"

Sierra was shaking by the time Axle turned back to her. "Axle…" Her voice was a panicked whisper, "I-is that true? Were warriors after you?"

Axle sighed, "It… it *is* true, but they only saw me and they lost control of their car back on the highway. They don't know who the others are and they don't know about this place."

"B-but what about you?" Sierra's lower lip started to quake.

"They lucked out with finding me this time; probably a slow night in the neighborhood and they picked up on my aura and decided to investigate. They probably don't even know who I am. Nobody even knows I'm *here*! As long as I keep under their radar then they'll never have a reason to look."

Sierra bit her lip and looked between him and Drake, "A-are you sure?"

Axle nodded and smiled, "Worst case: they bring me in—and me *alone*—on a few minor charges. No execution; just some served time or community service work. In the meantime, Drake can take my place and keep you and the kids safe and supplied."

Drake nodded, knowing Sierra just as well as Axle. "Until we know for sure how these warriors will respond to tonight, we'll keep our ears to the ground and stay out of the city. The next town is just a bit further out, so we can target a few of the smaller sites there to avoid heavy security and any added attention until we're sure this has all blown over."

"What did the other girl look like? You said one had blue hair, what did the other one look like?" Sierra frowned.

"Some platinum-blonde pit-viper of a vampire with purple eyes," Axle shrugged.

"You remember her eye color, Axle? I never remember *anything* like that!" Quinn grinned, "Has someone *finally* caught your eye?"

"Shut up," Axle rolled his eyes and looked at Sierra, "Why ask what she looked like?"

Sierra frowned, "That's Serena Vailean, the new leader of Clan of Vail. Please be careful around her, Axle; from what I've heard she's not one to be trifled with. She's still new to The Council's policies, so she's prone to aggressive and reckless behavior."

Axle nodded, "That certainly sounds like what we saw."

"Yea! She was a real bitch!" Quinn smirked.

"Language!" Sierra hissed at him, "I don't need the kids to hear those kinds of words. Things are rowdy enough around here."

"Sorry, Miss Sierra," Quinn pouted.

Axle looked over, startled by the sudden shift in Quinn's tone. It was moments like *that* that made him realize how young his comrade still was.

"Anyway, we've got to head back for the night," Axle sighed. "There's been a lot of activity at the subway and we don't want someone else staking claim to our turf."

"You can always come back here, Axle. You know you are always welcome here," Sierra frowned. "And I'd feel better if you guys weren't sleeping the streets at night after working so hard for us."

Axle shook his head, "We couldn't do that to you. It wouldn't be safe for the orphanage. As certain as I am that nobody knows we're here, I'd rather not take a chance with so much at stake." Axle smirked, "Besides, it's actually pretty cozy!"

Sierra rolled her eyes at that and Axle smirked before he nodded to the others to give them a moment.

"Bye, guys," Sierra waved to them, "Thanks again."

Lucas blushed and stammered his farewells.

Drake nodded back and herded the two down the stairs to join the others.

Sierra bit her lip and looked up at Axle, "About that Serena girl…"

"Look, don't let her concern you. Aggressive or not, she's just like any other clan warrior."

"I don't mean about the warrior part," Sierra bit her lip.

Axle frowned, "What then?"

"About what Quinn said…" She blushed.

"What Quinn…" Axle's shoulders dropped with realization and he shook his head, "Oh god, Sierra! No. No! It's *nothing* like that! I just haven't told Quinn about you and me; he's still got some puppy-dog crush on you and I don't want to start any tension that could impact us on the—"

"Then you *didn't* find her attractive?" Sierra frowned up at him.

It was Axle's turn to blush. "I… I mean, I guess. If you're into that sort of thing, I mean, but… like, I wouldn't—y'know—personally, and all—"

Sierra giggled, "You always were a bad liar." She sighed and shrugged a shoulder, "It's fine, though. I hear she's very beautiful, and there's no harm in looking, right? I mean, I look too."

"You do?" Axle raised an eyebrow.

"Mmhm. All the time," she giggled and swayed her hips in a brief tease, "Like that Shayne guy, for example."

A growl slipped from Axle's throat, "Shayne? That vulgar little pervert—"

Sierra giggled and pressed a finger to his lips, "Shhh. I was just teasing. I just don't like being alone in my jealousy."

Axle blushed at being caught and nodded, "Alright. That's fair. You got me." He paused, looking at her and wondering if he *should* take her up on the offer to stay. Finally, he took a deep breath and pulled her into a hug, "We'll be back soon with more. I promise. If something happens, you know how to reach me, and don't hesitate this time."

"I won't. And thank you."

"You don't ever have to thank me for this," Axle scolded her. "Though I *will* take a goodbye kiss if you're offering."

"Hmm… I don't know. Have you been a good boy?" She offered a coy grin.

"As good as a guy who steals from the rich to feed the poor can be, I suppose," Axle offered with a smile. "And speaking of stealing…"

With that, he swooped down and captured her lips in a passionate kiss.

Sierra gasped at the startling-yet-welcomed onslaught and wrapped her arms around his neck and pulled him down to deepen the kiss as she pressed her tongue to his. The sounds of her moans pushed Axle forward and he ground his hips between her legs. Gasping, Sierra wrapped her legs around his waist and she shivered as his hardening assets pressed to her core.

Realizing that they were nearing the point of no return, the two fought to tear themselves away from one another. Still panting from the effects of their passion, the two gazed at the one another as they willed their pounding hearts to calm.

"Someday..." Axle nodded, straightening himself, "Someday it'll be different for us. I promise." He ran his thumb across her swollen bottom lip and smiled as she nipped at his thumb.

"I know. I await the day," she smiled happily. "You'd better get back to the group before they begin to suspect the worse."

Axle rolled his eyes, "I'm sure Shayne's already telling some pretty tall tales in my absence."

"Then you'd better hurry before the tales get taller," Sierra offered.

Axle sighed, "You're probably right. Even your innocent words are beginning to heat my core." He offered her another quick kiss before forcing himself to turn away, "Until next time, Miss Sierra."

"Yes," Sierra sighed. "Until next time."

Starting down the steps, Axle spotted Drake waiting for him.

"I take it from the look on your face that Sierra and you had a little alone time again, huh?" Drake raised an eyebrow.

"Don't act so surprised," Axle frowned, "You... you didn't tell the others, did you?"

Drake rolled his eyes, "Like I'm sure they can't figure it out for themselves. But no, I didn't say anything."

Axle nodded his thanks, "You're a good friend." He sighed, "Someday, Drake. Someday I am going to buy her a ring!" He smiled, "Once we get enough money, I can help set the orphanage to be a nicer place and Sierra and I can finally be together."

"Axle... are you sure you want to put Sierra in that kind of danger?" Drake frowned, "You've amassed quite a reputation; earned quite a bit of enemies. You could risk putting her in a dangerous spotlight for those who'd want to get to you? And you know that she's not strong enough to stop them; she's not a fighter, and you'd be forcing yourself to *always* be a bodyguard first and a lover second."

"That's why I'm waiting," Axle looked down. "I won't ask her until I know that I'm free from that life. You know I wouldn't do anything to endanger her *or* the kids."

Drake sighed and nodded, "Well, I guess all we can do is hop, and I *do* hope for the best. I truly do. She definitely could use someone like you."

"I'm glad you think so," Axle laughed, starting towards the car to join the others.

Axle had gotten into the habit of parking the car several blocks down from the entrance to the subway, and though none in the group were unable to walk the distance it was clear that, though the body was willing, their minds weren't happy that their rest was being delayed.

All but Axle, who could still feel the electricity from Sierra's kiss racing through his veins. Stretching his joints, he looked around the others as they shuffled down the sidewalk; a wide grin growing as his therion instincts began to pull at him and he turned to the others.

"I'm going for a run. Drake, you want to join?"

"Nah. I'm going to pass out as soon as I get to my bed." He smirked, "Besides, as tired as I am, you're too slow for me when we run together."

Axle scoffed, "Sure, whatever you say!"

The others grumbled, wondering out loud how *anybody* who'd had the kind of night they'd had could have enough energy to even *think* about running.

Falling back, he watched as the five walked off into the subway and he sighed, about to pull off his shirt when he suddenly froze—hearing a rustling of movement—and narrowed his eyes in the direction of an alleyway across the street.

"Whoever you are, step out now!" He snarled. Almost instantly the tall, lean female stepped out and he let out a relaxed sigh, recognizing her instantly from her dark hazel eyes and short black hair. "Oh. It's just you," he turned his back to her as he finished pulling off his shirt. "Will you leave me alone already? I already told you: I'm not interested. Can't you just get the point and move on with whatever life you have?"

"Come now, that's not fair," the woman's voice was just as toxic as her scent. "This time I have a proposition for you. Please just hear me out."

He shivered at her voice and growled, turning to face her again, "Look, I'm not interested!"

"I just thought that—since you've clearly got something important that you're trying to do and have something of a law-problem—we could maybe help one another."

"If you think I'm *giving* you *any* of our earnings then you're crazy! Plus, I don't need your help. I've been able to do everything on my own already, what makes you think I'd need you?" He sneered.

"Well for starters" she glared at him, her purposeful stride driving her ever-nearer, "we can get this 'I' bullshit out of the way! While I appreciate a man who's willing to cover for his team, I think it more than insults our mutual intelligence to carry on such a ludicrous facade! Then there's the little matter of my fee: there is none! I don't want any of your so-called 'earnings'—though I feel the implications are rather preposterous given that they imply that you *deserve* any of what you've taken—nor do I think you're in a position to turn down my help considering the precariousness of your particular situation. What I'm offering you is *protection*—both from the preservers of the law as well as the breakers of it—and what I'm *asking* is for your *participation*."

Axle frowned and shook his head, "I'm not going to pretend to have understood *half* of the words you just said, Miss Thesaurus, but if what you're offering is real then what sort of participation are you expecting?"

The woman shrugged, "Every clan needs its members, right; its *warriors?*"

"*You...* you're a clan leader?" Axle frowned.

"You can't lead a clan of one," the woman chortled, "Which is where your participation becomes somewhat imperative to the process. You and I and the rest of your little group can be the beginning of something new; something that can—and *will*—take your little Vail problem out of commission. Wouldn't you agree that making supply runs to your little nursery would be easier with some *actual* support on your side? Wouldn't you agree that having your own clan to back you up would make things so much easier for your little girlfriend? Just think of it: a clean record from The Council, and enough power and strength to protect yourself, your crew, your lady, and all those little ones with no real home? Isn't that worth, at the *very* least, a moment of your time?"

"The jobs I take aren't exactly Council approved, what makes you think they'd agree for your *clan* to do these jobs?" Axle narrowed his eyes.

"I'm afraid that my willingness to sway your skepticism just ran dry. Now, you either take me up on my offer or I find somebody else who will! This is the final time I'll extend to you this offer," she frowned. "Make your decision."

Axle frowned, "My only chance?"

The woman nodded, "The choice is yours."

"Good. My answer is still 'no', so I guess this is the last time I'll have to say it, and none-too-fucking-soon either! Now if you'll excuse me, I'm going on a run."

"Ugh! You stubborn little mongrel! You *will* regret this decision! I promise!"

He watched as she spun on her heel and stomped off down the street, unable to hold back a laugh as she stumbled on the curb.

"Stupid bitch," Axle shook his head. "Must think I was born yesterday if she thinks I'd buy that much rubbish just because she talks like a damn dictionary!"

Sighing, he ducked into the alleyway to finish undressing and focused on allowing the transformation to grab hold of him. As his body shook and shifted with the excruciatingly liberating process, he gripped a nearby dumpster to keep his body upright. Breaking free of the confines of his human form, he let out a triumphant howl before he rushed towards the concrete wall in front of him and began a full sprint up the side. As his vertical climb lost momentum, he vaulted to the neighboring wall behind him—pivoting in midair to meet it head-on—and then repeating the act again and again until he'd reached the rooftops. Feeling the blood coursing through his veins like gasoline running through a V8 engine, he started across the blacktop, throwing himself over generator and in a forward summersault before landing in a tucked-roll that carried him back to his feet and an even more momentous sprint.

The humans were a clumsy and foolish lot…

But whoever had developed parkour had had the right idea!

This was the *only* way to run!

And while the bulk of his species enjoyed nothing more than ducking and weaving through the trees and brush of their natural habitat, there was no denying the potential thrill to be had in the urban jungle!

CHAPTER THREE
SOUL SOCIETY

AFTER THE NIGHT'S ORDEAL, SERENA and Zoey had finally made it back to the clan. Ever since the original headquarters that had been Serena's childhood home had been destroyed, they'd been forced to relocate. Fortunately, Serena's father had gone to great lengths to construct a secret underground facility in the event of an attack, and though the decision had been seen as somewhat unconventional, this bunker had been successfully expanded upon to allow for not only all the necessities and conveniences that they'd come to know, but an eerily vast sense of security.

After all, who would think to look for a complex clan of non-humans beneath a dense forest?

Isaac, already waiting at the entrance, hurried to Zoey's side and began to look her over. Serena sighed, rolling her eyes as Zoey's therion lover scrutinized over every bump and scratch.

"Really? We're only an hour late, for fuck's sake! She's fine,"

Serena chuckled. "No need to get your panties in a twist. Lord knows they're crowded enough already!"

"Serena!" Zoey's face went bright red.

"Oh, right! Like he doesn't know he's got a ballistic weapon in his—"

Enough! Zoey's psychic voice rang in Serena's head, silencing her in mid-joke. "It's alright, Isaac, really," she smiled warmly up at him and gave him a quick kiss. "We just had some car problems. Had to call for a tow."

"Yea, 'car problems'. That's one way to put it, I guess." Serena sighed, "You know that most of what was under that hood was custom?" She drove her fist into her palm, "I am *so* going to make those rogues pay!"

"Oh good! You guys are finally back," Nikki stepped out, her hair held up in a bun and her dark skin glistening from sweat.

"You'd better just be sweaty from an actual work out!" Serena narrowed her eyes.

"Yeah, yeah! We just got back from the gym." Nikki smirked. "No need to get your panties in a twist."

"Lord knows they're crowded enough already," Isaac chuckled.

"Oh, I bet you're just happy as a pig in shit to have had that opportunity, aren't you?" Serena stuck her tongue out at Isaac.

Both Isaac and Zoey laughed.

Serena rolled her eyes and sighed, turning back to Nikki and watched as Raith stepped out, still shirtless.

Serena stared. Though she knew that it wasn't Zane—not in the sense of who was driving the body, anyway—it was, day-by-excruciating-day, becoming a chore to not let that fact simply be forgotten. How simple would it have been just to let herself forget that the body she was staring at—the body she'd come to know and love—no longer contained the vampire she'd come to know and love? What she and Zane had had was, though based on a fleeting and chance encounter, far more meaningful than she'd even come to fully appreciate before it was taken away. Now that she was face-to-face with a walking, talking reminder of who had been taken away, the potential to forget that pain within the *actual* arms of who'd been taken was a throbbing possibility.

Except that it wasn't.

He *wasn't* Zane.

He wasn't hers.

And that hurt.

"Did you tell her what you found out, luv?" Raith asked Nikki; the faint hint of an Australian accent riding on his words and forcing Serena's boiling blood finally cool. It wasn't Zane's voice; it wasn't Zane's posture or gestures. Even his eyes had changed; the once silver and alluring right eye now showing as a dull brown, though the left was still the same blue that Serena remembered.

Serena frowned, "Did you tell me what?"

"What did you find out?" Zoey chimed in, stepping forward to join Serena at her side.

"It looks like we have some competition heading in," Nikki frowned. "Word on the street is there's a new clan in the works on the South side of town and The Council has already offered their support."

"Why the hell would The Council agree to *another* clan in *our* jurisdiction?"

Zoey frowned, "Do you think this is all in response to Axle and his gang?"

Serena growled, "This is bullshit! The damn file even said that he was a minimal threat!"

"The overall theme I caught drift of is 'added security'," Nikki offered. "Whether or not this Axle character actually poses a threat might not matter to them. Maybe they feel more manpower in their court will keep any *potential* plans to be reconsidered."

"Decrease the threat of crime by increasing the threat of punishment," Zoey nodded slowly.

"Fuck! As if there isn't a big enough turd on the goddam table, now they gotta invite Michael Moore to dinner?" Serena shook her head, "Between doing *our* damn job and trying to track down that Kristine bitch I'm not sure how I'm supposed to be expected to play the charming neighbor housewife."

"I'm not sure who in their right mind would see *you* as the charming neighbor housewife," Isaac frowned.

Serena glared at him, "Blow me, Donkey Dong!"

Zoey gave Serena a look, mouthing "Donkey Dong?" before finally turning her attention back to the group, "It may not be that bad, actually. Think about it: they can help us and that way we have a lighter workload. That lighter workload means you have more free time; free time that you can use to work on tracking down Kristine."

"And Zane," both Serena and Raith chimed in before looking at the other with a startled-but-appreciative stare.

Nikki bit her lip, "Do you really think that he's still... y'know, around?"

Raith nodded, "I really do. It's hard to explain, but being 'tied' to a person like we were for so long creates an undeniable bond." He shrugged, "I can't say *how* he's still alive, or *where* he is, but I know he's still with us and that the key to finding him is with that Kristine-twat. It would be nice to see my buddy again and actually have a chance to hang out like we used to, rather than just swimming around in his head."

Nikki bit her lip and looked away.

Though Serena wasn't happy about Nikki's reluctance to help them find Zane—to restore the *proper* owner to the *proper* body—it wasn't something she couldn't bring herself to understand. Though the details of their history were still unknown, Nikki and Raith *were*, at one time, very much in love, and though circumstances had removed Raith from his body and, Serena was sure, even seen an end to that body, they still had feelings that transcended the flesh. Though the turn of events were like something from a bad 70s sci-fi movie, the aura of Nikki's dead lover *was* now in control of the body of Serena's disembodied lover. Though everyone's effort to find and return Zane to his body was an undeniable priority, it did force Nikki to worry about what would happen to Raith's mind when things were restored.

And, though Serena was eager to have Zane returned to her—mind *and* body—she couldn't shake the crippling empathy of what it would do to Nikki.

"You alright over there, Ink-Doll?" Serena asked, giving Nikki a gentle shove.

Nikki smirked at the nickname and nodded, "Doing great, Goldi-fucks." She smiled and returned the shove, "Hey! Why don't you visit the clan tomorrow, Serena? You know, bring them some baked goods and introduce yourself. And by 'baked goods' I mean your typical snark and by 'introduce yourself' I mean remind them not to step on any toes."

"That'd probably be a good idea," Serena nodded and turned to the others, "I'm calling it a night for now though. See you all tomorrow!"

With that, she turned from the group and headed to her room, closing her inside her solitude and the only time she could ever let herself remember...

"Do you think she's going to be alright?" Zoey frowned, turning to the others as soon as Serena was out of earshot.

"She will be. It's going to work out. I know it." Nikki smiled, though Zoey could see the shift of pain clouding her aura. "Hey, I'm going to go take a shower and get some rest as well."

Raith grinned and started forward, "You want me to join you?"

Nikki noticeably wavered at the offer, but finally shook her head and took a step away from him. "I... We can't. It wouldn't be fair to Serena and Zane."

Raith's excited eyes sagged and he looked at his hand as remembering that he wasn't in his own body, "Oh... right." He shook his head, "Sorry..."

Zoey frowned and offered Raith a pat on the shoulder, "We'll figure this out. No matter what, we *will* make things right."

Raith nodded his thanks to Zoey before smiling at Nikki. "See you in the morning, luv," he leaned in and kissed her cheek—the only gesture they seemed to allow themselves—and headed towards his own room.

Zoey watched the two part ways, feeling an immense weight of sadness grow greater with every step that divided them. They had finally been reacquainted after such a terrible tragedy—a tragedy that even she had not been able to get Zane to explain in the many years they'd been together as colleagues and friends—but, despite regaining what they had lost, they forced themselves to keep their boundaries in respect to Serena and Zane, the two who had done so much for them both.

"Everything okay?" Isaac looked over, the nervousness in his eyes bringing Zoey back from her thoughts.

"Yea," she blushed, taking in the sight of him and feeling a calming warmth crawl over her, "I was just thinking."

"Thinking, huh? Isn't that that thing that turns your hair blue?" Isaac smirked and nuzzled her, "You want to head to bed as well?" Isaac's voice was a husky growl that crept up her throat and tantalized her ear.

"I'm... uh, not very tired," she confessed.

"That's okay," Isaac brought his carnal gaze to meet hers and smirked as he reached around and pinched her backside. "Neither am I."

Zoey squealed and grinned, turning to face her lover, "So what did you have in mind?"

"Let me show you!" Isaac scooped her up and carried her bridal style towards their bedroom.

Zoey giggled and smiled. She had never been happier before meeting Isaac, and, since the Vail Clan had opened its doors to therion members and taken in Isaac's pack, she'd no longer had to hide her otherwise taboo relationship and had been allowed to finally grow closer to him. Though the process of assimilating with the clan had come as something of a culture shock for Isaac's packmates, they'd looked to the two of them as a symbol that the union *was* possible; that vampires and therions *could* co-exist and even come to know each other as so much more.

It had given her a whole new degree of confidence.

Though Isaac still had some irritating concerns to work past:

"So... *a lot* of people have seemed surprised when they find out we're together. They say my kind can hurt others that aren't of our own kind. I was just nervous that maybe... you know, uh..." Isaac frowned, fumbling on his words, "I mean, I'd never asked before but... does being with me hurt you?"

"Isaac, baby, I'm a big girl, and I can handle you just fine. Trust me, you've *never* hurt me," Zoey smirked and pulled his head down and captured his lips with hers.

Seeming satisfied with the answer, Isaac kicked the door closed and he let out a fierce growl as he threw her on their bed and began to rip off Zoey's top. Crying out at the ferocity, Zoey watched as her lover worked her free of the confining articles that concealed her eager skin from his gaze and whimpered as his lips began to trace their way down her neck. Stalking further down, he captured a hardened nipple between his lips as he rolled the other between his thumb and forefinger. She cried out, arching her back in pleasure as he continued his teasing.

"Ah! M-more!" She gasped and watched as he began to kiss down her stomach. Not wanting to wait for him to rid her of her pants, she worked her shaky fingers to rid her pelvis of the denim so that his wandering kisses offered him the perfect view of her black thong when he'd finally arrived.

Seeing this, he grinned up at her, "You sure this isn't just dental floss?"

"I'll let you decide that!" Zoey shivered as she pinched her nipples in reaction to the sight of her carnal lover's bestial gaze emanating mere inches from her heated depths. Unable to bear the lingering torment of waiting for his touch, she hooked her legs behind his head and pulled. Though those of his kind had enough strength to easily resist far greater, he was easily guided into her core.

The feel of his tongue on her set her off and her hips raised as she let out a loud cry as waves of ecstasy began to tremor through her body.

Isaac looked up for a moment, letting his fingers continue what his tongue had paused, and grinned, "Ooh! So sensitive already?"

Unable to answer, she watched as he sat up, quickly ridding her of both her pants and thong before he began to slip out of his shorts. Stretching the waistband to its limit, he worked his semi-hard member into view.

Reaching out, she gripped his hardening length in her fist—her hand unable to reach all the way around its width—and marveled at how much remained on either side of her hand. "Oh my... it's so beautiful," she purred.

"Beautiful is not usually the term men like to hear about their—AH!" he growled in pleasure from the contact, instinctively thrusting against her touch and looking down at her, his fierce gaze watching her every move.

Feeling an erotic rush at the sense of the power she held over such a massive organ, Zoey shifted so that she could wrap both her fists around him—still grasping less than half of what he had to offer!—and began to pump her hands back and forth. She squeezed his member tight and he growled out louder. Moaning at the reaction she was earning, she grinned up at him, "But it *is* beautiful," she smirked. "I think you just need to reacquaint yourself with *true* beauty to understand what I mean." Pulling her hands away, she offered the tip of her prize a prolonged kiss before she lay back and spread herself.

"Mm... Now *that's* beautiful," Isaac smirked as he moved forward and pressed himself to her entrance.

Zoey groaned and nodded, thrusting her body forward and taking the crown inside of her. As the two began to meet the other's thrust, each of their moans carried the others and the two fell into a blissful union.

Zoey couldn't sleep...

Though sex with Isaac always knocked him out—any vitality within the therion was *always* spent after they'd reached their respective climaxes—it seemed the total opposite for her. Serena, one of the few people who Zoey felt comfortable discussing her sex-life with, had explained that she wasn't alone in this phenomenon. However, whether this had something to do with their being auric vampires and they were possibly draining some vitality in the coital process or if it was just one of those men-slash-women things had yet to be explored to any great extent.

"Who knows," Serena had shrugged off the question at one time, "maybe all women are a little bit vampire, huh? We're just *that* kickass!"

Serena...

Despite all her efforts to convince people to hate her, she was the nicest, strongest person Zoey knew. And though Serena's typical outward abrasiveness had only grown thicker and thornier since Zane had been taken, everyone that cared about her could see past it to the strong and loving friend who'd struggled against all odds to make things right for all of them.

She'd lost her mother and, in her pain and confusion, blamed her father and ran away from her home.

Loss.

Heartbreak.

She'd found promise in the arms of a human fiancé, Devon, who had been cast into the literal flames of jealousy by Kristine.

More loss.

More heartbreak.

She'd fought to maintain her strength and independence while bound to Devon's disembodied aura; an aura that, despite his sincerest efforts, warped and faded until a jaded and jealous shadow remained.

And then she'd met Zane, a vampire who'd seen more pain and loss than any should ever have to suffer in a thousand lifetimes; a vampire who had the terrible burden of delivering to an already shattered girl the news that her father—his beloved mentor—had passed.

More loss.

More heartbreak.

And in that moment—a moment where two broken and pained minds had come to cross paths—a bizarre and beautiful thing had happened: an accident that changed *everything*. Devon's body-starved aura had seen a chance in Zane's arrival; a chance to once again lie with Serena as lovers should. But, though the possession of Zane's body had blocked the night of passion they shared from the body's *rightful* owner, there was another mind present to watch their moment of passion.

An owner that was never meant to know love or pleasure or happiness.

Maledictus.

A monster—a curse!—that had dwelled deep within Zane and ripped free every time he lost control. And, in seeing Serena in the throes of ecstasy—a moment the curse had no way of understanding—it grew to love her; to, despite its most basic purpose, *not* kill her.

Serena had found purpose and promise in her new family with the clan that she'd inherited, and Zane had found the hope that he'd long-since given up on. And Devon, no longer human enough to see the promise of *true* happiness for Serena, had been extinguished in a jealous attempt to destroy Zane *and* the curse so that he could occupy the body.

Even more loss.

Even more heartbreak.

But the two broken souls had come to find strength in one another and in that support they were able to rebuild what they'd once been.

And in rebuilding themselves, they'd become one.

Until Kristine—still harboring the lingering rage of Serena's history with Devon—had returned to do to Serena what she blamed her for:

Not knowing of the other minds existing within Zane's body,

she'd ripped Serena's lover from his body.

Zoey shook her head.

How much loss could one soul handle?

How many times could a heart break before there was nothing left to mend?

Though even Serena may have believed that she was too callous of a bitch to feel any pain, those who knew her best could see that she was suffering.

"Serena…" Zoey whispered.

Though his aura still lagged with the weight of sleep, Isaac whimpered at the meek sound of his lover's sadness and rolled over, draping a strong arm around her waist and pulling her close to him. Blushing at his protective nature, Zoey nuzzled against his chest and reminded herself that, first and foremost, Serena was a fighter.

If *anybody* deserved pity, it was the ones that got in her way.

CHAPTER FOUR
LOVE IS DEAD

"SERENA?" A FAMILIAR VOICE CARESSED her skin with ghostly warmth and she opened her eyes as was met with Zane's mismatched gaze.

"Zane?" She frowned, biting her lip, "How are…?"

"Serena… I miss you. I miss you so fucking much," Zane frowned, sitting on the edge of the bed.

Serena sat up, still not sure what she was seeing.

Was she dreaming?

His form was hazy and seemed to be lit by his own personal source; the strange, white glow faded in-and-out over his face.

"I… I miss you too, Zane! I swear I'll find you soon! I swear! I've never stopped looking! Once I find that bitch, she's dead; she's fucking dead!" Serena whimpered, crawling to the end of the bed to join the spectral shadow of her lover, "I won't rest until I've found her."

"I know you won't, babes; even if I told you to move on and be—"

"No! I'm not giving up on finding you!" Serena choked on a sob.

Zane smirked and nodded, "See? Just as stubborn as ever!"

"Zane..." Serena felt a rock lodge in her throat and her eyes began to burn.

"Shhh. It's going to be alright," his voice was calm and a wave a reassurance rode on his words and rolled through her body.

She welcomed the feeling.

It *was* him!

Though she had no idea *how* he was there, this was all the evidence she needed that he was still alive.

That she wasn't crazy to still be looking for him!

"I've been at such a loss without you," she felt the first few tears roll over her eyes. "You goddam asshole! I'm not supposed to cry like this..."

The warmth and affection in Zane's eyes did not sway. "Don't worry. I won't tell anybody."

Serena laughed and clenched her jaw when she had enough control to do so, bringing her fist down on the bed. "Dammit! *That's* what I mean! I... I can't even stay *sad* with you there as... as..." She shook her head, "Dammit, Zane, what's happened to you? Where are you? Please... *Please* tell me where you are!"

Zane frowned and shook his head, "I'm... I'm not sure. It doesn't feel like a *where*; most of the time I'm not even self-aware enough to know *who* I am! Something just... something called to me now. I suddenly saw a path and knew that you'd be at the end of it." He shrugged and looked at his hands, moving as though he was about to clap and instead letting one hand pass through the other, "I actually *feel* like a projection of myself," he looked back up at her, "but it's worth it if it means I can see you right now."

Serena whimpered and shook her head, "It just... nothing feels the same anymore. I try—I swear I try—but I just feel so hollow and tired. I always feel so weak lately."

"Well, that's your first mistake! Come on, Serena," Zane's face widened as he grinned. "You weak? This coming from the cold-hearted bitch who beat the shit out of me less than two minutes after we first met? And now you're going to let *this* set you back?"

He cocked his brow, "The girl who'd blatantly ogled a picture of a man in a Speedo *after* we'd just fucked like porn stars feels lost without a single man? C'mon, babes, you could replace me in the time it takes you to bat an eyelash."

Serena bit her lip, "I... I never meant any of those things, Zane," she looked down, "Even when I joke like that now I... I feel like there's a fist in my gut. I feel like I never got to show you how much I really cared; how much I *really* loved you."

Zane shrugged, "I'd say this is a decent start." He smiled, "Just don't let me forget it when I get back, okay?"

"I'll *never* let you forget it," Serena smiled. "Even when I'm kicking your ass for being a loser."

Zane chuckled and shook his head, "Still a hardcore bitch," he gave her one of his looks, "You *are* tough, Serena. You don't need anyone's reassurance."

"How can you be so sure of me?" Serena felt a sting in her lip and tasted blood. Despite this, she kept chewing on it.

Zane frowned at the sight and shook his head, "Because you're too stubborn and strong-willed to *ever* be *anybody's* bitch but your own. Believe in yourself." He leaned back, "So what's new anyway? Raith treating my body well?"

Serena shrugged, "I guess. He goes the gym a lot more than you ever did."

Zane chuckled, "You were all the workout I ever needed."

"Ah, well in that regard the body is going without," Serena quipped. "As much as it seems to rub Nikki the wrong way—or not at all, I suppose—I've been making sure of your ongoing celibacy."

"Ouch. All those years being locked in my head and Raith's cock-blocked the minute he's out in the open," Zane pouted. "Let the poor guy take a swing at Nikki. I'm sure they could both use it; not like it's me in there anyway."

"It's *your* body!" Serena glared.

"Said the girl who let her phantom boyfriend possess and date-rape me?"

Serena blushed, "That... that was different."

"Not sure how," Zane chided her. "If all of this body-slash-no-body shit has taught me *anything*, it's that love transcends the flesh. My body is in the other room—my flesh and blood and organ..."

Serena raised an eyebrow, "You only have *one* organ?"

Zane shrugged, "Only one that you *wouldn't* sell on the black market for a new car."

Serena nodded, "Fair enough."

Zane rolled his eyes. "The point is, my *body* is in there... but this part of me—this... spectral, airy nonsense—is what you're after; what's making you laugh and cry and beat the shit out of my three-thousand dollar bed over."

Serena frowned and poked the mattress, "You paid three-grand for this?"

"*Maledictus* kept ripping up the cheap beds. Finally wrote a message in blood—though we never found out *whose*—on the walls of the main lobby that if we didn't upgrade then he'd destroy the city. Your father was pretty quick to special order that."

Serena sneered, "He always was a charmer. Not exactly missing him."

Zane looked over, "He hasn't emerged lately?"

"Not since..." Serena bit her lip.

"That son of a bitch probably only responds to *my* rage," Zane shook his head. "Those clever bastards!"

Serena frowned, "Who?"

Zane shook his head, "Don't worry about it. So how's the whole 'Clan Leader' role working out?"

Serena shook her head, "Like a jagged dump. The Council approved a new clan in town." She growled, "Bastards are coming in on *my* fucking turf."

"You tried pissing on a park tree yet? Y'know, if you're gonna play the whole 'mark your territory' game," Zane laughed.

"You're going to be a dick even like *this*?" Serena glared, "Don't think that just because I can't touch you I won't kick your ass!"

"Ha! There's the Serena I came to know and love! Good to see you are still in there," Zane smirked.

"There's nicer ways to console me. Just because a splinter in the balls is hilarious doesn't mean the laughter is the best medicine to fix it."

"Yeah, but you obviously don't love me for my manners. Just like I don't love you for your finishing school grades," he laughed, sticking his tongue at her. "So what do you plan to do with this clan?"

"I'm going to pay the assholes a little visit tomorrow. Show them not to fuck with me and all," she shrugged. "And I figured while I was visiting, I'd sneak around and see if I couldn't gather some intel on *exactly* why they've come to town."

"Oh? Why do you think they're up to something?" He looked over.

"Because the Vail Clan's been an established force in this area for *decades*! Then, only a few short months after *I* yank the title of 'leader' from my dick-hole, power-hungry brother, The Council green-lights a totally new clan to build just downtown?" She shook her head, "This is in response to *something*, and there's no way it has nothing to do with me or what we've been doing."

"What you've been doing?"

Serena nodded, "Some small-time rogue rolled in to town last week and everyone seems to think *that's* what's motivating this response. A whole new clan for *one* rogue; that sound suspicious to you?"

"Yea, it really, really does actually," Zane frowned.

"What do you mean 'actually'?" Serena glared.

Zane shrugged, the pale glow over his ghostly form shifting and fading slightly, "Only that you're rarely that logical. At least on the surface, anyway." He shook his head, "Normally The Council wouldn't waste resources for something like this; they'd just send one of their own if they felt the local clan was short-handed."

"That's exactly how I feel," Serena nodded, "but the others think it's normal and I should go say my introductions."

"You? Introductions?" Zane made a shuddering motion before turning back to her. "I'd like to see that!"

Serena blushed, "I... I wish you could see it, too"

"It's going to get better, Serena. You'll see," he smiled warmly and reached out to make a familiar motion. As his ghostly hand reached her chin, she raised her face to allow them both to believe he'd raised her face on his own. "Chin up, babes."

"Easy for you to say, phantom-Zane," Serena giggled.

"Oh you *know* I'm just as hot as the real thing," he stuck out his tongue and his body's glow began to fade again.

Serena bit her lip, "Unless I've finally gone crazy and you're just a figment of my imagination. Then you'd look however I'd want you to look."

"Nah, then I'd be here as Gerard Butler or Channing Tatum or one of those dry Hollywood queefs."

"See?" Serena cast an accusatory finger in his direction, "*That's* how *I'd* talk—though I'd *never* say an unkind word about my Tatum-tot...—anyway, that just proves that you *are* just a figment of my imagination!"

"Tatum...tot?" Zane shook his head, "Look, maybe we're just a pair of vulgar fucks who are too perfect for one another for the other to believe it could real," he scoffed. "God damn... You're still as beautiful as I remember."

"O-kay. Now I know that was something my mind made you say!" Serena laughed, falling onto her back and staring at her ceiling. "This has been a nice crazy-bitch dream."

"Maybe. Maybe not," Zane shrugged it off and smirked over at her, "Either way, I'm enjoying it, too, so don't wake up just yet."

She felt her cheeks heat and sighed, "Even like this you can make me blush!"

"You know you love it," he grinned.

"Psh! How could I not?" She laughed, turning to him as she began to reach out, "I promise to find you soon."

"I'll be waiting. For as long as it takes," he smiled and moved his hand out to meet hers.

She wanted his warmth.

She wanted his touch.

She *needed* him.

As their palms met, Zane's hand rippled and phased through her skin, the ripple traveling up his arm. As she watched, his form weakened—the pale light fading—and he drifted off like vapor vanishing into the air, leaving Serena staring at the empty edge of her bed.

Alone...

She shivered and fell back into the only warmth she could turn to and pulled the blankets over her as she nuzzled her face into Zane's pillow.

His scent would continue to haunt her until she found him.

Whimpering, she finally allowed the tears to fall freely.

"Zane... you son of a bitch! Where are you?"

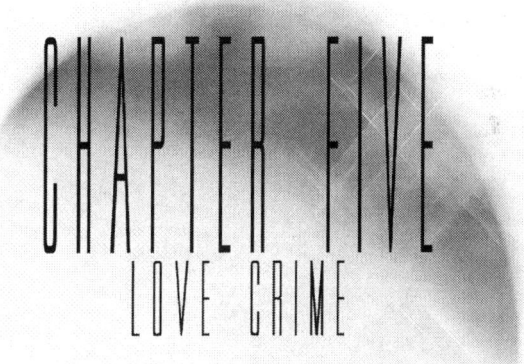

CHAPTER FIVE
LOVE CRIME

SERENA FROWNED, STEPPING THROUGH the automatic sliding glass doors—the motor groaning against the added pressure of her aura as she forced them to open faster—and stepped into the building that was to be the new clan's headquarters. She took a moment to look around the waiting room, the scene and décor offering the cover of a typical human office building, and scoffed.

This was the clan's headquarters? She hadn't even *talked* to the people in charge and she already wanted to line them up for a piece of her mind.

Smack. Smack. Slu-u-u-urp.

Serena suppressed a gag as she turned towards the secretary, the source of the repulsive sounds, and sneered.

Okay, they HAD to be messing with her.

"I swear to fucking Christ," Serena grumbled, "if I'm being Punkd right now I'm gonna tear Ashton Kutcher's heart out and eat it!"

"Ma'am—*smack slu-u-urp smack smack*—do you have an appointment?" The lanky sang girl perched behind a FAR-too-large desk called out to her. Starting towards her, Serena became increasingly aware of the *painfully* thick layers of eye make-up and neon pink lipstick as she blew an equally neon pink bubble of gum.

All of that artificial personality surrounded in two auras: a puke-orange cloud of overconfident air-headedness and a reeking-yet-invisible layer of syrupy perfume that must have come from the discount rack at K-Mart.

Pop!

"Oh I am *so* ready for supper, Ashton!" Serena growled and offered a silent prayer to whatever deity would listen that she wouldn't upchuck then and there.

"Ma'am?"

"Yea... uh, hi," Serena looked around again, shaking her head. "Kind of an elaborate hoax you guys are putting up here, isn't it?"

"Can I, like, help you with something?" She rested her bony chin on a palm with spider-like fingers that ended in fake nails painted with even *more* neon shades.

"How in the hell do you type with those things?" Serena couldn't hold back a disgusted sneer any longer.

The claws on the secretary's opposite hand began rattling an impatient rhythm on the desktop. "Do you, y'know, have an appointment or whatever?"

Serena blinked at the question, suddenly curious as to how many brain cells this creature must have lost in what she could only assume had been a lack of blood in her diet. "Uh. Yeah... I'm here to meet with whoever's running this joint. Pardon the phrase, but will you take me to your leader," Serena frowned.

"My... leader? *Smack pop pop smack*"

Serena suppressed the urge to tear out the girl's gum *along* with her tongue. "Yes. Your leader: the head honcho, the big cheese, the man in charge? Am I even making a dent here or is there too much neon paste caked in your skull to hear me? I'm from the Clan of Vail and we were informed that you would be assisting us."

More neon eyelid exposed itself as the girl narrowed her eyes, "Uh-huh. Well, let me just see if they're, like, available." The secretary turned to her computer screen for less than a second before turning back to Serena. "Oh poo. It looks like you, like, just missed them and junk. But I can *totally* leave a message for you."

"... just missed them... and junk?" Serena frowned, feeling her temper begin to rise, "And you, *like, totally* don't know when they'll, *like*, be back... *and junk?*"

"Nu-u-upe," the rhythmic clacking started up again along with an increased rate of chewing, "But I'll totally tell them that you came asking for them," she snapped another bubble with her gum. "I'm sure they're, like, *sooo* wanting to meet Vail Clan Barbie and all."

"Listen up, Play-Doh ho! I'm about two red cunt-hairs from leaping this desk and leaving my own personal message for your bosses with your insides. So here's how this is going to work: I'm going to, *like*, not kill you—'cuz I'm feeling generous... and junk—and you're going to keep that dead meat you call an ass planted on that chair while I go upstairs and check for myself. In the meantime"—she leaned over the desk enough to turn the computer monitor on—"I'll let you start a personal list of all the ways you just proved all of *this*"—she gestured to their surroundings—"to be every bit the *joke* I knew it was!" Serena began to turn away from the large desk and headed towards the elevators as she heard the secretary hit a call button.

"Security!"

Before Serena could cross the distance to the secretary to rip her head off, two large therions stepped into the room and took her at each arm, dragging her towards the automatic doors.

"Really? Is all this necessary?" Serena growled. "I only came to speak with your clan's leader! If anybody should be getting dragged out it should be My-Little-Bone-Me bitch back there!"

"The Leader's out on business at the moment. Try back later," one of the guards said.

"Once you've had a chance to cool down," the other finished before pushing her through the doors.

Serena growled, catching herself as they threw her out the doors and raised her middle finger at them.

"Up yours, you limp-dick fuckers!"

"I knew there was a reason I liked you!" A familiar voice called to her.

Turning, she spotted Axle and rolled his eyes, "You've gotta be shitting me! All this nut-fuckery over you showing up in my town and you just—*plop!*—hang out on the new clan's goddam doorstep?" She shook her head, "Axle Travers, the elusive therion rogue! Goddam joke! You know what? Fuck it! You and they can go suck a dick! I'm going home!"

"You remembered my name?" Axle smirked, "The infamous Serena Vailean honors me."

Serena glared, "On second thought, kicking your ass might just be the perfect thing to vent my mood right now!"

She started towards him and sighed as he smirked and turned to run, heading into the alleyway neighboring the clan's building.

"Really, numb-nuts? That's a dead end!" Serena scoffed and rushed after him, only to find the alley empty. "What the fuck?"

"Up here, buttercup!" Axle called from above her, where he was hanging upside-down from a fire escape rung that he'd locked his knees around, "You're probably going to want to up your game if you want to vent that mood of yours!" He laughed and pulled himself up and over edge of the ladder, and jumping to the rooftop.

Serena smirked, "All right, you spritely fuck! Time for some fun!" She jumped onto the fire escape and began to climb up to the roof.

Axle was sitting on the opposite corner of the roof by the time she arrived. Smirking at the sight of her, he lifted his left arm and pressed the watch around his wrist to his ear.

"I think my watch stopped…" He mock-pouted.

"Your pulse is next!" Serena took a step towards him.

As her foot landed, Axle did a back-handspring that returned him to his feet. Seeing that speed *was* a factor, Serena decided to cut the play short and simply use her vampire speed to cross the rooftop before he'd even had a chance to blink. Unfortunately, before she even had a chance to shift her focus into overdrive, he'd already taken advantage of a nearby antenna, which he vaulted over to clear the distance to the next rooftop.

Accepting the obvious challenge, Serena smirked and rushed across the rooftop in overdrive and using the superhuman speed to propel herself after him. Once her feet left the roof, the laws of physics took hold and the once time-frozen world came alive as she dropped out of overdrive to avoid watching the world—and her airborne leap—pass by at a snail's pace. Slamming onto the other roof, her boots skidded with the excess momentum and she overshot Axle, who'd banked to the left to allow her to pass.

"Decent moves," he offered, already standing on the roof's ledge. "Though that 'faster than a speeding bullet' shit won't do much good in a game where *jumping* reigns supreme."

"Game?" Serena panted, the exertion from jumping in-and-out of overdrive so quickly already taking its toll on her vampire system. "Since when is me kicking your ass a game?"

"No no," Axle wagged a finger at her. "You see, you kicking my ass is the *prize* you win. The game, however, is parkour."

"Huh?"

Axle pouted, "You know, parkour? Free running?"

Serena tapped her toe, "So *jumping* reigns supreme in the game of free *running*? Tell me, you didn't think this banter through all the way, did you?"

"Probably not," Axle shrugged. "I was too busy planning out the part where my buddies snuck up behind you while I was *delivering* the banter."

"What?" Serena threw up her aura in a defensive shield behind her as she spun to face off against...

A vacant rooftop?

"Oh you have got to be shitt—" Serena sighed, "You're already gone, aren't you?"

Turning, she confirmed her suspicions, spotting Axle already sprinting across the rooftop two buildings ahead. "You cheap little shit!"

She began to rush after him once more. Jumping across each building at the pace he did; neither gaining nor losing a pace on him as they entered a more urban area. As the rooftops became less and less flat and more littered with rises and ladders, however, the capacity for Axle's notorious elusiveness became that much more evident. Every time that Serena thought she had a drop on the therion, he'd throw himself between a railing gap or flip from a ledge only to land in mid-sprint like a cat on a beam no wider than his arm. Though combined agility and speed threw off Serena, who found herself forced, again and again, to compensate for a missed opportunity at grabbing him by fumbling across a light post or catching herself on a balcony.

Finally settling into her own groove, Serena focused less on trying to capture Axle and more on simply keeping up. The hunt soon became a chase, which soon after that became a test of skill.

Serena no longer cared if she got to feel her knuckles against

Axle's jaw; she just wanted to prove that she wouldn't be so easily eluded.

And Axe—judging from the excited swirl of his light-green aura—knew it!

If Serena made a move to gain height on him, Axle would find another path to end up right beside her; if she tried to take the low path to increase the obstacles, he'd not only meet here there, but expertly dodge and roll over everything in his path.

Winding up side-by-side in a full-sprint along a pair of scaffolding beams at a construction site, the two leapt into the air and freefell for eight stories before landing on the roof of a meat-packing facility. Serena stumbled, her bowing her knees to cope with the force of the landing while Axle hit the roof in a tucked roll that carried him several meters ahead and allowed him to roll gracefully to his feet.

Panting, he turned to face her and offered a nod, "You're good." He smirked and shrugged, "But I'm still better."

"Whatever helps you sleep at night," she grinned back, trying—and failing—to not look as winded as she was. "Where'd you learn to move like that anyway?"

He frowned and, obviously confident that Serena was done chasing him, plopped himself Indian-style on the roof, "I grew up on the streets; a ward of The Council's so-called care, which pretty much meant I got to come-and-go from whatever establishment they tried to plant me in. Let's just say that when it comes to caring for abandoned youths, our people aren't exactly on the ball." He shrugged, "Anyway, when you're always being chased down for this or that—either because somebody caught you stealing something or because they realized you'd jumped their gates a few weeks earlier—you learn how to run. And when the people you're running from are people like you, you learn how to run *faster*."

Serena frowned, feeling a familiar tug of pity at Axle's story. "I suppose that's true enough," she sighed and, deciding there was no point in pretending she still planned to chase him, followed his example and sat down; her left knee pulled up to her chest. "Most of the therions I know focus more on strength than speed, though." Serena sighed and looked over at him, "Have you always been on your own?"

"You suddenly interested in me for more than just the warrants on my head?" He grinned.

Serena frowned, "Would you rather I just shot you?"

"You have a gun?" Axle raised an eyebrow, "Where the hell would you keep it?"

"Wouldn't you like to know. So you gonna answer my question or not?"

Axle frowned and shrugged, "I was a part of a pack at one point, but we were attacked by hunters. Only me and my friend got away, and when we were found wandering the streets by a warrior we got thrown into our first orphanage."

"Not much to say for grammar lessons, I see," Serena chuckled.

Axle stared.

"Nevermind," Serena frowned, noticing his aura darken under the weight of his memories and she found herself wanting to help him more than she was driven to arrest him. Shaking her head, she pulled herself to her feet and towards him—holding up her hands as a peace offering when he noticeably pulled back—and took a place next to him. "Look, there's two ways we can do this..." She began.

"Oh? What are we doing?" He gave her a sidelong glance.

"Definitely *not* what you're thinking," she sighed.

"And what would you know about what I'm thinking, fang-head?" Axle scoffed.

"Because"—she held up a fist and let her pointer finger rise—"one: I might be a blonde, but I know that *anything* with a dick between its thighs is thinking the *same* thing—and since your kind are notorious for being *mostly* dick, I'd say that counts further for you—and two:"—she let her middle finger spring up to join the first—"I might be a 'fang-head', but I'm *also* part auric and I can *read* your thoughts with greater clarity than an Ernest Hemingway novel."

Axle's face reddened and he nodded, "O-okay. Fair enough... so what are my two options?"

"You can either *allow* me arrest you NOW—willingly surrender to the Vail Clan so that I can use that to our mutual advantage--*or* you can explain to me what your entire gig is aiming at and, if I see a point behind it, work with you to make things right."

"My gig"? Axle frowned.

Serena nodded, "Yea. Like, *why* you're running around my town stealing money of all things. Don't get me wrong, I'm sure you're a real asshole in your own right, but you just don't seem the selfish type who steals for no reason."

"I see," he frowned and looked down. "If I let myself get arrested, there's a chance that you won't be able to help me, right; that The Council would just take me away?"

Serena nodded, "That's what makes it a risk, sport."

Axle nodded slowly, "If—and this is a major *if*, mind you—I'm willing to show you what I've been doing, can you trust me long enough to show you?" He looked over, determination set in his face.

Serena frowned. She *wanted* to trust Axle, though she couldn't fully come to grips with *why*. He didn't seem like the enemy that the files she'd read had made him out to be, and she wanted to find out more about him before she made the decision view him as a danger.

"Okay," she sighed and nodded. "Fine. You have my trust. Now what are you going to do with it?"

Axle grinned and stepped over as she heard the sound of cloth ripping and gasped, seeing that he had ripped his shirt.

"What the hell are you doing?" She glared, "This *was not* what I agreed to."

"Then I guess it's a good thing that *that's* not what I'm doing," he shook his head and started to tie the torn cloth around her eyes and she frowned, moving to pull the blindfold off. However, her wrist was caught by a strong grip and she felt warm breath near her ear.

"This stays on until we get to where we're headed."

Serena frowned, "How do I know you're not just gonna lead me over the edge of the roof?"

"*That's* where the trust part comes from," Axle's voice chimed. Then, as an added quip, "Sport."

Serena frowned and nodded as she was suddenly lifted in the therion's strong grip and she gasped as her cheek met with the expanse of his chest. He was stronger than she'd thought, and, as he started running with her in his arms to wherever it was he was going, she found herself feeling far more comfortable than she was comfortable admitting.

CHAPTER SIX
I WRITE SINS, NOT TRAGEDIES

SERENA SIGHED AS AXLE FINALLY let her down and she bit her lip, hoping the blindfold would come off soon. Their trip had landed her in what must've been the convertible she'd been "introduced" to the other night. As Axle's mystery trip took her further and further, she began to worry that Zoey might send a search team after her. She was sure that she'd been gone longer than the others would have expected, and if Zoey couldn't pick up on her auric signal she might assume the worst.

"We're here," Axle finally announced as he pulled off the blindfold.

Serena blinked at the sudden flood of light and frowned at the sight. The building he'd taken her to was old and abandoned and off in the deep, dark seclusion of who-knew.

"Oh good," she rolled her eyes, "you're going to show me

where you hide the bodies!"

"I'll have you know that *this* is what passes as a *decent* mythos orphanage," Axle shot as he climbed out of the car and waited for her to follow. "Come on. The children will be excited to meet a newcomer anyway."

"An orphanage?" Serena looked at the building again, "It's... uh, kind of a dump."

Axle glared back at her, "Yea. Almost like it could use some *money* to pay for the cost of supplies to fix it up, huh?"

Serena bit her lip with realization and followed after him. "Why haven't I heard anything about this? Wouldn't The Council have something to do with this?"

"Because The Council's investment in childcare is limited to what they've *approved* of, and they're rather *disapproving* of rogues who try to dodge them. The kids here were all unfortunate enough to be born to parents who worked *very* hard to *not* exist on The Council's radar. According to your higher-ups, none of these kids *exist*." Axle growled and shook his head, "And, if they don't exist, then they don't need the little luxuries like decent shelter with running water and power, food and *legal* sources of blood for the vampires, and medical supplies. Which means that those luxuries come from those willing to do what needs to be done," he looked over, "like *stealing* and *running* from those who would get in the way."

"I..." Serena stared up at the building, unable to even begin to think of a response. All the crimes she'd seen on the files, robbing mythos blood supplies and medical facilities; cases of kidnapping and turf warfare. All of it—every single crime he'd been charged for—suddenly made sense. "This entire time..." Serena shook her head in disbelief, "Y-you've been taking care of *them* this whole time..."

Axle nodded, "I couldn't be sure if you'd understand, so I needed to keep this location secret before I could show you where I've been bringing everything we've stolen."

With that, he pushed open the door.

"AXLE!" Serena gasped as a small boy, a sang with a bright blue aura that danced excitedly around him, rushed forward and jumped into Axle's arms. "I knew you'd come back soon," he boasted.

Serena frowned, noticing that the boy only had a single fang.

"Oh come on, Fang, you know I can't stay away from you kids for long," Axle smiled. "Where's Sierra?"

"Miss Sierra was reading us a story, but I heard your car and I snuck out!" Fang grinned and turned to face Serena.

Serena blinked for a moment as he squirmed free of Axle's arms and ran over to her, squealing in excitement.

"H-hi," she smiled, looking down at him, I'm—"

"I know! You're S'rena!" He grinned, "I heard stories about you from my mom and dad!"

"Your parents?" Serena blinked and hoisted the boy up, allowing him to cradle against her shoulder and looking over at Axle.

"Fang's sort of a unique situation," Axle explained. "His parents *were* properly filed with The Council, but they weren't credited or insured to any clan. They wanted to lead a safe, quiet life, but…" He trailed off, offering no other explanation than a shrug.

Serena nodded, "Always a gap in the system." Biting her lip, she looked back at Fang, "I'm so sorry about your parents, hun."

"Yeah, they got killeded by hunters. Mom and Dad weren't strong like you, S'rena. They told me bedtime stories about you; told me that you were a strong warrior and that you came back to Vail to save us! And now you've come to help Miss Sierra!" His smile widened as he bounced in Serena's arms.

"Oh wow… I-I had no idea there were stories about me," Serena blushed and then looked down at Fang. "But I only came back to Vail a few months ago. When did your parents…?"

"Not long ago…" Fang whimpered and looked down sadly, "Axle saved me and killed the hunters!" He looked back at the blushing therion, "He's *real* strong too, S'rena!"

Serena looked up at Axle and smiled as she gave Fang a tight hug before setting him down and starting to look around the orphanage.

The place was an undeniable shit-sty!

There had to be something she could do to help.

Though she knew it would take some sizable paper-pushing and tweaks to how she filed cases with The Council, she was certain that Zoey would know how to work the system in their favor so the children and any who were working to help them could be brought into the Vail Clan. It would certainly ruffle a few feathers initially—getting *that* many unregistered mythos kids suddenly filed into the Vail system *would* earn more than its fair share of dirty looks—but they deserved another chance and even if The Council didn't approve right away.

And even then, they owed Serena *big time* for dealing with her scheming brother, who would've turned their entire organization inside-out if he'd had his way.

She had them by the balls, and she'd use that grip as leverage to prove to them that the children were worth it.

After all, she'd never been against busting the balls of authorities; why should the most influential authorities of all be any exception?

"Axle? Why are you here again so early?" A timid feminine voice called out and Serena looked up to see an equally timid sang woman with long black hair and bright green eyes step out; the numerous eyes of many, many children peering out from behind her.

"Sierra," Axle smiled, starting towards her, "This is Serena."

"I know who it is," Sierra frowned, "The question is *why* you brought her here? Her knowing of us could get us all into trouble with The Council!"

Serena frowned as she wondered what the orphanage had to do with Axle's stealing until it finally clicked.

"I already know that he's been stealing to help you and the kids?" Serena nodded, stepping forward.

"Yeah! He's our Robin Hood!" Fang grinned.

Serena smiled, "He is, Fang," she looked at Sierra and offered a reassuring nod, "And I'd like to help him. I'd like to help all of you." She looked around, noticing several different types of mythos, and smiled. The Vail Clan would *definitely* be livelier, and it was exactly that liveliness that Serena looked forward to. Seeing Sierra's aura shift but still retain its skeptic rigity, she went on, "I'm not to say anything about your personal Robin Hood *or* this place." Serena smiled. "I believe that what you are doing is right," she shrugged and smirked, "and I don't report things that are right to The Council. They're politicians; they only care about that sort of stuff when it makes them look good." She winked.

"You... are you serious?" Axle's eyes widened.

"Yeah, what of it?" She glared back, "Even the big, bad law-girl Serena can have a change of heart, can't she?"

He laughed and nodded, "I suppose so, and if you can then you must not be *that* bad." He smirked and motioned to Fang, "Though it looks like you've taken my hero spot in Fang's eyes."

She smiled, noticing even Sierra's aura and posture relaxing; her defensive frown quickly growing into an excited smile.

"You're welcome here anytime. However, it's the kids' bedtime, so maybe you could stop by earlier next time? We could all sit down and read a story together."

Fang bounced in Serena's arms still and looked up at her, hope filling his eyes as he waited for her response.

"It's a date," she laughed and set Fang back down and turned to Sierra. "It was very nice to meet you, and thank you for doing all of this."

Sierra smiled and nodded before turning and waving to the kids who all ran forward and surrounded Serena in a tight group hug.

Serena cried out as the group slammed into her, forcing her to use all her strength to remain standing as she laughed and tried to calm the frenzy with head rubs and high-fives.

"Ahh! Crazy little beasts, all of you! Go on! Get to sleep!" She laughed as Sierra went about trying to herd them away.

She watched as they slowly began to pull themselves off of her and rushed to the stairs. Fang still stood a moment longer and she smiled, stepping over and giving him one last hug. "Sleep well, Fang. I'll see you again soon," Serena smiled warmly.

Squealing out an excited-yet-indecipherable response, the little vampire turned and followed after the others.

"Who would've thought that *you* would actually have a soft spot for children?" Axle laughed.

"You want a soft spot in your fucking skull?" Serena quipped, still unable to take her eyes from the heartwarming scene of Sierra guiding the kids to their room.

"Uh oh," Axle cackled, "the bitch is back!"

"Oh, I'm sorry. Did me showing a moment of kindness tarnish my image to you?" She laughed. "Let's go. I need to get back to the city."

"Right," he smiled and, though Sierra and the kids were far beyond earshot, called out his farewells as he waved before leading Serena out and hopping into the car. "Come on, princess!"

Serena laughed and jumped in as well. "Princess, huh? I like that!"

Serena smiled as the convertible came to a stop on the side of the road that bordered the woods, and Axle looked over at her once more to flash her a grin of his own.

"Thanks for coming today, Serena... *and* for being so understanding. You have no idea what a relief that represents for all of us."

"Yea, well, you were just lucky to catch me on one of the few nights when I'm *not* hungry for the flesh of innocence, I guess." Serena sighed and looked off towards the woods; towards the Vail's hidden headquarters, "I want to help you—all of you, I mean—and I think I know how to do it, but it's going to be your turn to trust me, okay?"

"You don't need to get involved like that. Just help us by keeping this a secret. Please," Axle bit, taking her hand in his and Serena blushed, feeling the tingling warmth his hand held.

"Keeping *what* a secret, Serena?" Zoey stepped out of the darkness and approached the car.

"Zoey..." Serena sighed, "I figured you'd start looking for me sooner or later."

"Serena! He's the one we've been tasked with *arresting*! You can't just be having a moonlight drive with him!" Zoey frowned.

Stepping out of the car, Serena extended a psychic *Just go. I'll handle this and meet up with you later,* to Axle. No sooner had she shut the door behind her then Axle had peeled off, leaving a wide-eyed Zoey to watch the taillights grow smaller with distance.

No dawdling or hesitation. *Exactly* what Serena had been hoping for.

"No!" Zoey threw her aura out in an attempt to stop the car, only to have Serena deflect it with her own.

"What are you...?" Zoey glared over at Serena once more and finally let out a long sigh, "I *know* that you miss Zane, but we can't have your wild side coming back out like this."

"I know that, Zoey. I do! I just..." Serena bit her lip and shook her head, "Do you trust me?"

Zoey frowned, looking back towards where the last of Axle's taillights had been seen. "I..." She sighed and stomped her foot, "Dammit, Serena! You know I do," she growled and shook her head, "I don't always *understand* you, but I *do* trust you. We just don't want to cause anymore trouble for our clan."

"Of course not! And *that's* one of the things I'm working towards, but I need you to let me—and me *alone*—deal with this Axle situation, okay? This could be big—very big!—for all of us!"

Zoey looked over quizzically, "Should I be worried?"

Serena laughed, "When should you *not* be worried. By the way, I'm giving you tomorrow off."

"Huh? What for?" She frowned, looking over and bit her lip.

"Well, I couldn't help but notice that you've been, well, walking straight and all. Which can only mean that Isaac and you haven't had *nearly* enough alone time lately and your lovey-dovey stares in the clan are getting old!" Serena smirked, "Go have some fun tomorrow and don't come back 'til you *and* Isaac's horse-dick are both in wheelchairs, okay?"

Zoey sighed, "You know, all this teasing about Isaac's—"

"Zoey... are you about to try and tell me that your boyfriend *doesn't* have a monster in his pants?" Serena cocked her head to one side.

Blushing, Zoey stammered for a moment before finally grumbling and offering a nod.

"Exactly!" Serena patted her friend on the shoulder, "And while I'm *dying* to know how Isaac's gone this long without splitting you up the middle like a piece of firewood—I'm sure your vagina is like some sort of dimensional gateway, right? Like, a doorway to a new world where you can just store untold lengths of heaving, throbbing—"

"Serena!" Zoey's face was beet red.

"You know, for somebody dating a guy who could put Tommy Lee to shame you're awful bashful. You should work on that. In fact, those are your only two jobs tomorrow: not turning into a blushing schoolgirl at the mere mention of hefty spurting cocks, and dealing with Isaacs"—she gasped and cupped her hand over her mouth—"hefty spurting cock!"

"Serena!" Zoey smiled warmly. "Thank you so much! That's so sweet... well, in your own twisted, perverted way, I mean."

"It's no problem, girlfriend. No need for us all to be working non-stop anyway." Serena bit her lip.

Zoey looked over, picking up on some residual psychic signals. "We'll find Zane soon, Serena! Then we can all be whole again."

"I know, Zoey. Thanks," Serena smiled weakly even as the threat of tears grew, "I...I just hope we find him soon."

Zoey looked up and frowned, "Serena... you're crying."

"Nah! I just... I-I got myself jealous with all that talk of he-hefty, spur—O-oh fuck, Zoey..." she felt her knees buckle and give out under her as all the stress, all the commotion, all of the new information, and, through it all, Zane's ongoing absence hit her hard and she began to sob. Falling to her knees in the streets, she let herself finally break down in Zoey's presence and finally accepted her friend's support fully.

Zoey was quick to drop down beside her, throwing her arms around her and pulling her into a tight hug. "Serena! Oh my god, Serena! It's okay! It'll be alright! We're gonna find him! I swear to you, Serena, you'll have him back! You'll have him back!"

"I just... I miss him so much..." Serena whimpered, finally letting the last of her defenses collapse in the arms of her friend. "I miss him so goddam much!"

CHAPTER SEVEN
THE LIGHT I SHINE ON YOU

"COME ON, ZOEY! ARE YOU ALMOST ready?" Isaac called frown down the hall.

Zoey, giggling at his excitement, glanced over at Serena as she finished getting dressed. "Can you tell him I'll be done soon?"

"On it," Serena poked her head out, "Hey! Hold your horse-cock! Rushing her isn't going to make her go any faster! She's a girl, not a Pomeranian!"

Zoey held in a chuckle.

Though, Zoey hadn't expected Serena's breakdown—hell! Serena hadn't even been expecting it—it appeared that letting it out had brought a new sense of understanding and closeness between the two. With this renewed vitality in their relationship, they'd both felt comfortable further discussing their plans for the Vail Clan and finding Zane.

Shaking her head, she finished applying the last of her makeup and threw on the high-heeled boots that Serena had lent her. She grinned at her outfit, ogling her reflection in the tight black dress, thigh-high fishnets and black leather boots.

"Damn girl!" Serena smirked, "Your boy's gonna flood his damn socks before you even get out the door!"

Zoey giggled and nodded, "Well, let's see if you're right."

As they started down the hall, they watched Isaac's eyes lit up.

"Wow... I mean... well, no. 'Wow' pretty much sums it up," Isaac gawked, making no effort to hide the stalking of his eyes as he took in the entirety of her new look.

Smirking at his reaction, Serena nudged Zoey with her hip and used her aura to push her forward. Zoey stumbled—not yet used to the heels—and fell into Isaac's arms.

Exactly as Serena had planned.

"Serena," Zoey's accusatory tone was broken by her giggles.

"Oops, sorry," Serena chuckled and shrugged. "Thought I saw a loose thread. By the way, Zoe, I gave Isaac permission to use my motorcycle for tonight," she winked, "so good luck keeping that outfit in one piece while he's enjoying the torque."

Isaac grinned.

"You... you gave him *permission* to drive *your* bike?" Zoey bit her lip and looked over at Isaac who just grinned.

Isaac smirked, taking Zoey's hand and pulling her towards the garage, "She also gave me access to some of the clan's extra funds for our date."

"Oh my... Thank you so much, Serena!" Zoey smiled warmly as Isaac hopped on Serena's metallic purple Kawasaki Ninja.

"Hop on, Zoey!" Isaac grinned as he patted the extra space in the back of the bike and handed her the only helmet.

"What about you?" Zoey pouted.

"Please," Serena laughed, "A therion's skull breaks every time they transform! What's a few cracks here-and-there when a quick freeing of the beast will heal everything?" She smirked, "Speaking of 'freeing the beast'..." She winked at Zoey, who quickly pulled the helmet over her head to hide her blush. Glancing over at Isaac, she shrugged, "Sorry I couldn't find a helmet big enough to fit the head that matters, stud."

Isaac rolled his eyes, "I'm starting to think that all your jokes are just envy."

Serena gasped, "You *just* figured that out?"

The two laughed.

"Oh please…" Zoey's muffled voice rolled out from under the helmet, "Please let me live to see the rest of our date!"

Isaac barked a loud laugh. "You'll live," he glanced back to ogle her a moment longer, taking a few extra moments to linger on the plunging V and the ample cleavage it made visible, "Though I can't make the same promise about your dress."

With that, he kick-started the bike and gave the engine a few revs, letting the bike come to idle

"Oh!" Zoey shivered as her knees shivered, "That feels… different!"

Serena chuckled, "Looks like she's already on a slow simmer, Isaac." She gave them a wave, "Better not waste any more time!"

"So, where are we going anyway?" Zoey called forward, keeping her arms wrapped tightly around Isaac's waist as he navigated the streets.

Though his driving wasn't nearly the erratic roller coaster ride that Serena always provided, there was still the thrill-inducing speed and potential for danger that, though she'd *never* admit it to either him *or* Serena, always got her pulse racing.

"I thought we could start off with a dinner and then maybe take in one of those shows I keep hearing so much about?" Isaac responded, "And I've already reserved the luxury suite at the Hyatt."

"That sounds wonderful!" Zoey smiled.

"That was so much fun!" Zoey giggled as Isaac carried her across the threshold of their luxury suite hotel room, "You know, for as long as I've lived here I'd *never* been to one of the shows here!"

"It *was* pretty spectacular, huh? And that steak!" Isaac licked his lips as though there might have been a trace that he'd missed at the restaurant, "By far the *best* steak I've ever had! And I've eaten actual livestock!"

Zoey laughed, "You beast."

Isaac grinned, "Don't sell yourself short! You were eyeing me like a main course halfway through the show there, baby."

Zoey grinned as Isaac laid her back on the bed and crawled over her, catching her lips with his.

She gasped and wrapped her arms tightly around his neck, pulling his body down on hers further as she wrapped her legs around his waist. Finally, he was able to break the kiss and he grinned down at her body.

"I told you this dress wouldn't live the full night…" He growled and took the front of the dress between his teeth and ripped it straight down the middle, letting his lover's assets bounce free of the shredded fabric.

Zoey gasped and tried to force an insincere pout, "Aw… I liked that dress!"

"Then I'll buy you another one," he grinned, running the tip of his tongue up the valley of her breasts that had been teasing him all night until he reached her throat. "Just so I can rip it off of you again."

"Oh! You vicious beast!" Zoey laughed, patting at his strong chest, "Then I guess it's my turn!"

Isaac looked at her, confusion washing the lust from his face. "Your turn?"

Zoey grinned and her eyes turned fierce as she threw out her aura and snared Isaac's clothes; ripping them to shreds and letting the scraps fall across the bed in a tattered heap. Spotting a strip of fabric that had once been a part of his t-shirt, Zoey grinned, lifting it with her aura and wrapping it around his eyes.

"Oh! You *are* dirty!" Isaac laughed as Zoey pinned him to the bed with her aura.

"You haven't seen anything yet!" Zoey smirked and began to trace her lips down his neck, running down his broad chest, to his stomach and, finally, what lay beyond. She grinned as she wrapped her mouth around the head and started to work down his shaft.

"Oh fuck! Zoey! That feels amazing!" Isaac reached down and placed his hands on top of her head, running his fingers blindly through her hair.

She moaned, pausing long enough run her tongue across the full length before filling her mouth once again as she reached into his mind with her aura and began a similar treatment on the pleasure centers of his brain; intensifying the sensations while simultaneously flooding his mind with scenes and images that flashed behind the darkness of his blindfold. The process earned a howl of pleasure from her lover, who pitched and writhed in response to her efforts. As her combined efforts and the lingering effects that her outfit had had on him over the course of the evening grew more overwhelming, she felt a familiar and telltale throbbing.

Only then did she free his member and his mind and pull away.

"H-huh?" Isaac whimpered.

"Don't worry," Zoey smirked and moved over his lap, slowly beginning to lower herself over him, "I'm still here."

Isaac growled in pleasure as her heated wetness enveloped him, and he quickly moved his hands to her hips and pulled her down onto him. Crying out together, they soon fell into a steady rhythm as their bodies united.

"I love you, Zoey!" Isaac growled out.

"Mmm! Isaac, I... I love you too!" She purred as she let herself sprawl against the chest; rolling her hips and drawing twin sets of pleasured moans until...

As her orgasm rolled over her, Zoey pitched her body back and frantically pumped against the source of her ecstasy. Nearly halfway through her peak, Isaac howled and clamped onto her hips as he joined her in a moment of mutual bliss.

CHAPTER EIGHT
THE HAND THAT FEEDS

"WHAT'S GOING ON, MAN? YOU'VE been different ever since you came back last night." Tristan frowned as he leaned forward on the makeshift couch they had made from found cushions and various sized crates when they settled into the abandoned subway station.

Axle looked over at him and sighed.

He didn't want to admit it, but Tristan *was* right...

Since the night before, he couldn't get Serena off of his mind. She was fun and unpredictable and so much more spontaneous than anyone he had ever been with. He knew it was wrong to feel this way, especially when things with Sierra were...

He bit his lip as his stomach knotted, and, after taking a deep breath, he turned to face Tristan.

"Just a lot of my mind, I guess," he smiled.

"I would imagine you might. Sierra said that you brought that Serena-broad to the orphanage last night." Drake glared, "Why in the hell would you trust her there? Did you forget who she *works* for?"

"What? He didn't! He wouldn't!" Quinn frowned and turned to face him, "Axle! Tell them you wouldn't do that!"

"She's not like the others!" Axle blurted and almost instantly regretted it.

How could he know that? He had just met her!

This little obsession had to end, he realized.

And he had to end it soon!

"You're right; you're all right," he nodded. "I shouldn't have brought her there. I was smart enough to blindfold her so she'd never see the location, but I'll be more careful from now on."

The others settled as he explained this, and he inwardly shuddered at the lie he'd brought himself to tell. Though he'd been *very* careful to keep the location of Sierra's orphanage a secret on the way *to* the location, he'd hadn't replaced Serena's blindfold—hadn't even made the damn effort!—on the trip back. The reassurance, however, seemed to settle the others' concerns, and though a part of him felt stupid for having so easily trusted another, he couldn't shake the feeling that Serena was still different. Standing up, he started towards one of the storage rooms that he had claimed as his bedroom.

"I'll see you all tomorrow. Sleep well, guys," He smiled and tugged at the rusty door to the room until its position somewhat resembled "closed".

Run, dog—stupid dog, run now! Run!

Growling at the masculine whisper, Axle reached for the light switch. Pulling the small metal chain, he was startled by a small hand that emerged and grabbed his wrist. Growling, he hit the light switch and pinned the figure to his bed. "What the fuck do *you* want?" He glared down at the woman from earlier, "I thought you were done following me around."

Impossible. No other smells... nobody else.

"Oh, wouldn't you have liked that?" She grinned up at him.

Growling, Axle shook his head and pulled away, knowing that the threat of death wouldn't phase this woman, who seemed to know that he could *never* bring himself to kill anybody. Looking around for the owner of the male voice he'd heard, he realized that it was just the two of them in the room.

"What are you doing here?"

No! No saving—no—them—no saving—if you don't—saving them if you don't—RUN!

Axle clenched his teeth, pressing his thumbs into his temples and trying to ease the throbbing pain in his head.

"Wh-what?"

"You didn't think that I was going to be done with you *that* easily, did you?" Her eye twitched and she swatted at the air, "Shut up, will you!"

Axle stepped back, not sure what he was witnessing. "I didn't say anything, you crazy bitch!"

"I wasn't talking to you, you idiot," she sighed and glared at him, "I'm not even here *for* you. Well, not for your sake, at least."

Something that sounded like breathing made Axle look over his shoulder, but nothing presented itself.

"Who else is here?" Axle demanded, glaring at her, "Why *are* you here?"

"Who else is here is none of your concern!" She smirked, "And I'm here to make good with my promise."

"Promise? What promise?" He frowned, beginning to ready himself for whatever was about to happen.

Stupid dog; dog's so stupid! Wanna run—gotta run!—won't run when he's told!

A strange tickle grew behind his left ear and he moved to scratch it.

It moved to his right...

Wanna run—gotta run!—won't run when he's told! Dog's so stupid; stupid dog!

He growled, "Who the—"

"I'm here to make you regret your choice, and to get what I'd been asking for since the beginning. Is any of this igniting *anything* resembling a memory in that dense skull of you—Dammit! Will you *shut up!*" She stepped back and swatted about for a moment before seeming to suddenly remember Axle was still watching. Clearing her throat, she sighed, "I'm here to kill you, of course!"

Her eyes narrowed on him and his feet were no longer touching the floor.

Stupid dog; dog's so stupid!

The invisible force holding him squeezed the air from his lungs and he gasped, unable to call to the others; unable to make any sound at all!

Wanna run—gotta run!—won't run when he's told!

"Wh-who…" he croaked out right before the hold launched his body HARD into the storage shelves behind him. Crying out, he fell to the floor as the shelves collapsed and dumped their contents on top of him.

"All this… because I rejected you?" He coughed and some blood spilled out in the process.

"I guess you could say that I've never been one to take rejection lightly," she sneered. "We all have our flaws, puppy-dog, and I've never claimed to be perfect."

No saving them now…

The woman tilted her head towards the other side of the room and Axle's body followed the gesture; sailing through the air and crashing into the wall. He cried out as the invisible force pinned him against the cold metal wall; pushing down on his body and forcing the air from his lungs.

Fucking aurics!

Unseen energy fields and power-draining holds and mind-reading nonsense…

Nothing to fight against.

But he was never one to follow logic!

Fight it, dog! Fight it, dog! Fight it, fight it, fight it!

"I'm not a damn dog!" Axle growled.

The woman frowned, "What did you say?"

Axle growled and began to struggle against the auric hold; working the oxygen-starved muscles in his body to start his transformation even under the pressure of her binds. His body strained and rippled with the beginnings of the change, but something in his mind popped and a high-pitched whine grew in his head until he was forced to stop the efforts. All at once his transformation ceased—his muscles going unresponsive—and Axle looked up in anger as the auric began to laugh.

"I don't think so!" She hissed, holding up her hand and clenching it tightly. As her fist began to shake, the tightness seemed to carry over to his body and he felt several of his ribs begin to crack under the pressure. "And now you die!" She laughed and began to twist her fist, only to have the rusted storage room door thrown off its hinges.

Then it was her turn to be thrown across the room.

"Tristan!" Drake motioned towards the woman, "Deal with her! Keep her busy! Lucas, help me get him down!"

Bind her! Bind her mind! Tell them! TELL THEM! Bind her NOW!

Axle groaned as Lucas reached out with his hand and suddenly the hold on him broke free, allowing him to fall to his knees. Wrenching, he coughed up a wad of blood and cupped his arm across his chest, fighting against the broken ribs to speak.

"B-bind... bind her! Now! Her mind!" He nodded to Lucas, "Help him!"

Lucas frowned, "B-but you're hurt..."

"NOW!" Axle hissed in pain and he doubled over.

"I can deal with her," Tristan called back, "Mend his injuries while I deal with—"

The auric's body was thrown through the wall and he cried out in agony. The woman stood, regaining her composure, and as the others started towards her a shimmer of light—a wave; a shimmering ripple—rocketed outward and slammed them all to the ground.

Axle growled—the rumble in his chest reverberating through his cracked ribs and cutting his breath short—and fought to start towards his friend. Before he'd even taken a step, however, the invisible force suddenly slammed into his face, caving in his skull.

Too late, dog.

Stupid, stupid dog.

No saving any of them now.

"NOOOOOOO!!" Axle roared, his rage cutting past the torrents of agony wracking his body. "You bitch! You will pay! You *will*!"

"Have you seen yourself?" She laughed, "You're in no position to be—What the hell?"

Lucas stood and squared off against the woman, "You... you hurt my friends."

The woman scoffed, "Oh darling... I intend to do so much more than—"

The usually shy and reserved auric let out a yell that shook the very foundation of the subway station; his hair whipping about his head as he unleashed what felt like a tornado in the small room.

The woman fought to keep her footing as the force of Lucas' anger threatened to topple her over, and as her struggles kept her distracted Lucas turned his focus towards Axle.

"Keep... you safe..."

Axle frowned, opening his mouth to speak only to be swept up in Lucas' auric whirlwind.

And then the young auric collapsed.

The woman scoffed, straightening herself, "Stupid kid. Very, very stupid!"

"What did you do to him?" Axle growled.

"I didn't have to do a damn thing," the woman chortled. "The little retard blew his own fuse." She kicked Lucas' body, "Try to do too much at once and... POOF!" Shrugging, she stepped around him, "Happens to the weakest of us, I'm afraid. Now... to kill you."

The woman's hand raised and, once again, tightly clenched. Axle bit his lip, feeling a flare of energy around him and then...

Nothing?

"Dammit! That stupid, self-sacrificing dimwit!" The woman kicked Lucas' body again.

Axle blinked. She couldn't hurt him? He looked down at Lucas' body and bit his lip.

Keep... you safe...

"Lucas... no."

The woman sighed, "I think this one had a bit of a boy-crush on you. Looks like you're shielded, and, 'cuz Lady Irony is an obvious bitch, it looks like *that's* what killed him," she chuckled. "Well, if I can't kill you then at the very least I just get both of you nuisances out of my hair!"

"Both...?" Axle looked up.

Holding out her hand, she began to focus on her palm— staring as though something of substance was resting there, but Axle's eyes weren't trained to see it for whatever it was. After a moment, she slammed her hand into his forehead and a wave of pain grew in his head and he cried out as his vision began to fade.

Then there was only one name—one face—that occupied his howling mind.

"SERENA!"

CHAPTER NINE
THERE AND BACK AGAIN

NIKKI SMILED AS SHE LED RAITH towards the small café that had become her down-time hotspot. Plopping him in one of the chairs at one of the few available tables that occupied the outside of the café, she smiled.

"Now you stay there, and when I get back you'll get to taste the *greatest* espresso you've ever had."

Raith raised an eyebrow, "You realize I've *been* to Italy, right?"

"Silence, non-believer!" Nikki held up a hand as she stepped inside. Though the place was bustling with activity, the bulk of the orders had already been placed and, smiling at her own good luck, she was able to get the coffees and a scone with hardly any wait.

Returning to the table, she presented Raith with one of the steaming cups and the warmed sweet-bread. "Ta-da!"

Raith smiled, "I missed you so much, luv."

Nikki rolled her eyes, "Nonsense! I was only in there five minutes... *tops*!"

"You know what I mean," Raith chuckled.

"I... I know. I missed you too..." She smiled softly and bit her lip, "I just wish that..."

"I know," Raith sighed. "Zane was my best friend..." He shook his head and bit his lip, "Don't take this the wrong way, but I wish I'd've told you to piss off when you asked us to do that job..."

"I know... but it wasn't your fault, or even Zane's! *I* didn't know how bad things had gotten," she looked down, "there was no way I could've known how bad things had gotten. But all of that—the taroe tribe and that awful *Maledictus*—are all in the past now, and once we find Zane and set things right then everything will be better." Nikki sighed as she smiled softly at him. "Besides, things will get better soon enough. I can feel it."

"That's what I've always loved about you, Nicc'oule," Raith smirked and allowed himself to lean back—one of the first acts of *true* relaxation that Nikki had seen from him, "You've always been so positive; always feeling things could get better."

Nikki felt her cheeks heat up. It had been so long since she'd heard her true name, and hearing it brought their previous history flooding to the surface of her mind. Reliving those times, however, drove her to remember what had happened to them, and she shivered.

"I... I'll admit that being upbeat hasn't been easy without you," she confessed. Taking a sip of her coffee, she looked up at him, "Do you... ever think about it? What happened, I mean?"

"I try not to. The memories of you and I—*those* I appreciate; in small doses, at least—but..." He shook his head, his body tensing again as he leaned forward in his chair. "Zane might not be in here with me—with us"—he shook his head—"make no mistake, whether or not *Maledictus* is active doesn't mean he's not still in this body, as well—but the body still *remembers*. It's like, all of our combined memories of what happened are stored in here for that monster to use for whatever he likes."

Nikki smiled, taking his hand in hers and squeezed gently. "You can tell me anything you'd like. I'm here for you. Maybe talking about it will help."

Raith frowned, "I'm not sure..."

Nikki bit her lip, "Please. I need to know what happened to him—what happened to you—after what my people did to you two…"

"Raith? RAITH?" Zane thrashed against the binds and hands that held him against the frigid stone slab, "G-get off me! GET OFF! WHAT THE FUCK ARE YOU DOING TO HIM? RAITH? RAITH!"

The blood curdling cries of his friend were all the evidence Zane needed to know that, whatever they were doing to him, it wasn't something he'd want to see. Fully registering this, however, he couldn't bring himself to stop his struggling against his captors to see past them; to get a glimpse of what the taroe chief was doing.

It wasn't supposed to have been like this!

It was just a job!

A simple job!

It was never supposed to—

There was a pause in Raith's cries—a bitter-sweet break in the pained howls—that was occupied by a jagged and tortured hiss as Raith struggled to inhale.

"YOU FUCKS! YOU SICK FUCKS! LEAVE HIM ALONE, OR I SWEAR I'LL RIP EVERY ONE OF YOUR—AHHHH!" The cold that had begun to seep into Zane's core was flooded by scorching pain. Fighting against the leather bind that held his head, he pushed to see the source.

Then suddenly wished he hadn't.

The dagger was nearly buried to the hilt; the few inches still protruding allowing him to see the rusted and serpentine metal that had been embedded in his belly.

"Silence that wretch," the chief's voice rose over the celebratory jeers of the taroe tribe. "I'll tolerate no more of his flapping tongue!"

"Shall I carve it from his head?"

Zane wretched and whimpered as the dagger was yanked from his guts and a length of intestine followed.

Raith's cries were stifled then, the chief letting out a grunt as he fought to maintain control of the therion.

"No," the chief's voice oozed with malicious intent, "he'll suffer far more if we allow him to keep his voice. Here, use these."

Zane whimpered as he felt the warmth of his insides begin to worm down his hip. "What... what do you want from us? Wh-what—"

A pair of hands seized his face and forced his lips open as another taroe leaned in and pushed two fleshy lengths into his mouth. The taste of therion blood—*Raith's* blood!—rolled over his tongue before it seeped down his throat. His vampire body ignored the bitter taste of the source and excitedly compelled Zane to seek out more, but his awareness of who the blood belonged to made him wretch. As his bound body quaked with spasms of nausea, he felt a pair of hardened points rake against his lips.

Claws...

His eyes widened and a muffled cry squeezed around the two fingers that had been cut from Raith's hand.

"I think the filthy blood-sucker *likes* it!"

"Disgusting creatures!"

"One of you help me," the chief called out. "This wretched dog won't keep his eyes open!"

As a few of Zane's captors stepped away from the blood-covered stone slab he'd been secured to, Raith's cries started up again.

~One Day Earlier~

"Oye! Zane!" Raith's voice carried over the excited din of the pub, "Zaney-boy! Quit dickin' around! I've got us—"

"Calm down, Raith!" Zane chuckled and nudged one of the drunks he'd invited to his table, "Can't you see that I'm entertaining company?" He laughed again.

Raith frowned, his nostrils flaring as the stink of liquor flooded his sensitive nose. "Company?" He shook his head, quickly turning back to Zane, "We ain't got—"

Zane shook his head, "You're being rude, my friend! I've told these gentlemen all about you *and* our adventures! Come, sit and drink with us! I'm certain they'd love to hear your news!"

Raith frowned, but begrudgingly pulled a free chair from a neighboring table and sat beside Zane. "I hope that you haven't told them *everything*!"

The others cackled.

"Yer friend's got a bit of a speech impediment there, eh Zane?" One of the drunks smirked, picking up on the lingering traces of Raith's accent.

Zane shrugged, "That's right, boys! Raith here is a true-blue Aussie; a genuine product of the great 'Down Undah', isn't that right Raith?"

"Well why doesn't he throw anotha' shrimp on da bahbie and join us for a drink?"

They all cheered.

"I bet he can drink you 'undah' the table, eh?"

More laughter.

"Not a chance! Nobody can hold their liquor like Zane!"

Somebody at the bar scoffed, "Wasn't always that way."

"Oh yea…" a pair of skeptical eyes fell upon Zane, "I remember when you couldn't even handle a beer and a shot without passing out. What the hell happened to you?"

Zane shrugged, recalling how often he'd passed out or become sick during his visits to the bar before he'd been turned. Since becoming a vampire, however, no amount of alcohol could faze him, and his reputation among the patrons he'd grown up with his entire life had quickly been replaced. Though none of them knew what had caused this bizarre change.

And they never could know.

Forcing a grin back to his face, he shook his head, "Nuh-uh. We all have our secrets. Now, if you'll excuse me, I think my partner has earned a private moment."

Pulling himself to his feet, Zane made a note of faking a stumble followed by several shaky steps before seemingly regaining his composure and making his way, with a few unsteady sways, to the front door.

By the time the two of them were outside, Raith was shaking his head.

"Again' drunken'onsense; all tha' *really* nec'ssary?" He rolled his eyes.

Zane shrugged, "Do you have any idea how much I've been drinking?" He shook his head and laughed, "Those American bastards are probably shocked I'm still *alive*!"

"You shouldn't be drinking with them at all!" Raith's head was swill swaying back and forth.

"Well that's rude," Zane mirrored the gesture, "Just because they're human?"

"There is no 'just because'! It is *exactly* because they're human," Raith's voice, though kept low, carried a heavy weight of severity that struck Zane as though it had been shouted in his face. "You're *not* one of them anymore, and you never will be again!"

Zane frowned, "You know I didn't choose this life."

Raith shook his head, "Well this life chose you! And there are *rules* that you'd better be ready to follow if you want to go on having any kind of life! For starters: *not* letting humans see that you're not one of them!"

"But I grew up with these people," Zane chewed his lip. "They've known me my entire life!"

"Your entire *human* life," Raith corrected him, "Who you were is not who you are now, and those people will forget all about who you *were* when they see that you're not aging like they are."

Zane felt a growl rumble in his chest but fought to keep it in as he forced himself to turn away from the pub. "So what is it that you wanted to tell me?"

The excited smile that Raith had been wearing when he'd first entered the pub returned then.

"I got us a job!"

"I still don't understand," Celine called from the door, "Why exactly do you suddenly have to leave for the weekend? I thought we had plans?"

Zane didn't need to turn around to know that she was frowning at him.

And though he didn't boast any psychic abilities, there wasn't a doubt in his mind that her arms were crossed and her jaw was locked.

Sighing, he finished packing the last of his supplies and secured his bag before daring to turn around to face his fiancé.

Her arms were crossed.

Her jaw was locked.

And, as an added bonus, she was tapping her foot.

He sighed again. He didn't care how dangerous the job Raith had gotten them was; it was certain to be a cake-walk in comparison to that moment.

Assuming Celine let him live long enough to get past the door...

"Look," Zane set down the bag, being gentle to not let his knives rattle and draw attention to their presence—he wasn't sure which was worse, Celine getting more nervous about his need for weapons or the potential for her to get more upset and *use* them. "I know you wanted to go out, but this job is big; *really* big!"

"What sort of job is it?" Celine's face shifted to concern and Zane felt the first wave of guilt hit him.

"It's..." Zane sighed and sat on the bed, "Well, it's not entirely legal. I guess it's—"

"'Not entirely *legal*'? Zane, what are you getting mixed up in? Does this have anything to do with that Raith-dog again?"

Zane sighed, "Don't call him a dog."

Celine glared and took her first few steps into the room, "I *knew* it! That mongrel's been trouble for you since the day you met him!"

Zane narrowed his eyes at that, "He *saved* my life! If it hadn't been for him, the vampires who turned me wouldn't have left enough to wake up!"

"So when is your brain going to wake up, Zane? Just because some stray therion showed up in time to chase off some delinquents doesn't mean you have to be his best friend, and it *certainly* doesn't mean that you need to tag along on his little—"

"Enough," Zane kept his voice low, but the anger towards her words drove the single demand with enough force to achieve the desired effect.

Celine stopped.

A painfully silent moment drifted between them, making the distance that much more obvious.

Zane looked at her, taking in the beautiful vision. She was

hardly made-up for the quiet evening in, but, in her rawness, he saw exactly what he'd fallen in love with. Wild, copper-red hair and blue-green eyes as deep and promising as ocean waters; she was a wild flower of a sangsuigan vampire.

He truly loved her.

And that was why he needed Raith's jobs; jobs that brought power and wealth.

Jobs that would secure him with an official warrior status and enough money to promise her the kind of life he wanted to offer her.

She would never understand how much that sort of life meant to him—what that sort of life could mean for her—and she'd never see the jobs as anything more than a reckless danger. She'd turn down the offer of the "fairy tale" life just to keep him from taking on the jobs.

Zane sighed and rubbed the back of his neck.

Maybe there was more to it than the power or the wealth...

Maybe it was the thrill...

Maybe he needed—

"I just don't want to see you hurt," Celine finally offered.

Zane blushed and, finally, nodded. "I know... but this is important to me. I need you to understand that. And Raith *is* my friend—my *best* friend—and I can't *not* be there when he needs me," he sighed and looked down, "Please understand..."

Another long silence.

"You're taking our weekend," Celine scolded him.

He nodded, "I know, but I'll make it up to you."

Her fingers captured his chin and raised his face to take her in. As she came into focus Zane became aware that she was no longer wearing her blouse, and as her pert, puckered assets appeared at the level of his eyes he could no longer bring himself to worry about anything else.

"Oh... Evening, ladies, I wasn't expecting to see you two out and about tonight."

Celine giggled and pressed her breasts closer towards him, "They're disappointed to hear about you leaving this weekend, too."

"Oh my," Zane frowned and offered a nervous glance upward, "You don't think they've told the kitty yet, do you?"

Another giggle slipped free before Celine adopted a stern

expression and shook her head, "I can't make any promises. Word travels fast in these parts."

Zane whimpered in mock-guilt, "Maybe I should talk to her myself..."

Celine nodded, "Perhaps you should," she leaned in and slammed her lips to his before moving her mouth to his left ear. "Just remember that she's hard of hearing; be sure to talk *real* slow, and don't forget to annunciate clearly."

Zane smirked, "Oh don't you worry about that, dear," he wetted his lips as she joined him on the bed, "I'm a truly cunning linguist."

Raith checked his surroundings for easily the hundredth time as he pulled himself onto a ledge on the cliff and slunk into the familiar chasm. Though it was too dark to see through to the other side, he'd navigated this particular passage enough times to know to duck his head eight paces in—the jagged stalactite that had been the cause of many previous night's headaches rustling through his hair as he passed underneath—and braced himself for the sizable step down that indicated the halfway point to the secret cave.

Their secret cave.

Before he could even see her, he could see the glow from her tattoos. Though she'd offered on several occasions to explain how the ink of her people's sacred tattoos worked, Raith had refused to let the magic be explained as anything but just that.

Magic.

Just like her.

"I thought you wouldn't come," Nicc'oule's voice echoed all around him in the small cave.

Raith smirked, "Really?"

"No," Nicc'oule giggled, the intricate, body-shaped network of glowing tribal shapes that was Raith's only clear view of his lover bobbed towards him. "I was certain you'd be here sooner or later. I just hate waiting."

"They say it's the hardest part," Raith chuckled.

"Do they?" Nicc'oule's hand brushed the crotch of his pants

and she cooed at the find, "I don't think they were waiting for the right thing."

Raith chuckled and brought his hands to Nicc'oule's hips, pleased to find that—as he'd suspected—she was already naked. With her tattoos' magic glow illuminating her, he took a moment to quietly appreciate her dark skin and all the splendors it had to offer before locking his gaze on her own and kissing her.

Unfortunately, though it hurt him to pull himself away from what they'd already begun, the visit was, first and foremost, one of business.

Nicc'oule's tattoos faded slightly as he stepped back and she offered a solemn nod as she retrieved her jacket. As she shrugged her naked body into the garment—a sight that Raith felt was even more distracting—she focused her powers towards an oil lamp that they kept in the corner and the small cave was soon awash in light.

As Nicc'oule's features came into focus, Raith felt another tremor of regret at having broken the embrace with such a tantalizing creature. Everything about Nicc'oule reminded him of earth; her strength, her fluidity, the deep, dark richness of her brown skin and the perfect, flowing mane of black hair that framed it all. She was built every bit as beautiful and powerful as a panther with all the mystery and majesty of moonlight in her enchanted tattoos.

And now he was expected to ignore all of *that* to talk business…

"So…" Nicc'oule leaned against a large rock, "I suppose things worked out then?"

Raith nodded, pausing on the rock and recalling the many times that he'd laid Nicc'oule on top of it in far less serious encounters. Remembering how she'd looked below him on those occasions made him realize how impatient he was to get the formalities over and done with.

"I'll have to pay my friend out of my own pocket just to get him to come along, but it'll be worth it," he explained.

Nicc'oule frowned, "He doesn't know the truth?"

Raith shrugged, "As much of it as he needs to. If he thinks we're being paid by some wealthy, faceless members of some hoity-toity vampire clan to rob from your tribe, then he won't see a problem with it."

"But if he knew that you were doing it as a favor for your

lover...?"

Raith nodded, "Then he'd be worried about me and try to talk me out of it. Look, he's a good friend; he'd rather think we were stealing from the taroe because somebody he's never met is greedy. He's trying to save up some money for him and his lady, anyway."

"Then wouldn't he understand your need to help *your* lady?" Nicc'oule frowned, clearly unsettled by the conditions.

Raith shook his head, "Then he'd want to know why my lady was asking us to steal from her own people; something that *I* can barely understand!"

"I told you already," Nicc'oule stepped away from the rock, "this relic is"—she shook her head and tossed her hands into the air—"I don't know, Raith, it's evil; just *evil*! The damned thing seems to have put a dark cloud over the hearts and souls of all of them and every day it sits on that shrine they just seem to sink even lower because of it! That thing *needs* to be taken away, and I hope once it's gone you'll destroy it before it has a chance to poison you or anybody else."

Raith nodded, "You won't have to worry about that. Zane and I have done plenty of jobs like this—easy in-and-out robbery—and as long as Zane sees his cut of the profits he never asks any questions about who has what we stole."

Nicc'oule bit her lip, "So how much are these 'mystery clients' paying him, exactly?"

Raith shook his head, "I don't want to tell you that."

"Oh?" Nicc'oule frowned at him, "*That* bad, huh?"

Raith nodded, "Bad enough that you might not let me finish this boring talk and bend you over that rock."

Nicc'oule glanced over her shoulder at the site of countless other romantic encounters and smirked, "My... that *is* bad." She nodded and slipped out of her jacket, her tattoos beginning to glow again and the lantern's light suddenly snuffing out. "Well then, I'd say it's best if you don't tell me."

"So how did Celine take the news?"

"How do you think she took it? She nearly boiled my balls!"

Raith laughed, "You get kicked out of the bedroom?"

"Well, not exactly," Zane chuckled.

Raith paused and looked back at his friend.

Zane felt his smirk betray him.

Raith shook his head, "Tell me that I didn't indirectly get you laid!"

"I would," Zane shrugged, marching past him, "but that'd make me a liar."

The two laughed as they sprinted towards a vertical rise of the mountain. Launching themselves into the air, they planted their feet along the rock and used their remaining momentum to sprint to the jagged ledge nearly ten-meters above them. Reaching the point first, Raith grabbed the lip of rock—willing his arm and hand to transform into its clawed, bestial form to offer better grip—and looked back in time to see Zane about to miss the mark.

"Little help!" Zane called out as gravity began to pull him back down the mountain.

Catching his friend by the wrist in his free hand, Raith shook his head and grinned down at him, "Being post-coital going to be a problem? I can't be catching you all day, you know!"

"Shut up and pull me up," Zane grumbled. "We can't all have been born to mothers who weren't ashamed to fuck mountain goats!"

Raith raised an eyebrow and let his grip loosen enough to let Zane slip several inches. "It was a puma, actually."

"Whoa! WHOA! Alright! I'm sorry! You're part puma! YOU'RE PART PUMA!!"

Still laughing, Raith pulled him to the ledge and they continued up the mountain towards the isolated village of the taroe tribe.

"As we draw nearer to the peak," Raith explained, "we're going to begin seeing more and more glyphs. From what I've gathered, these are meant to channel the right energies into their village while blocking out the bad. While all this jargon doesn't mean a thing to us, we can at least gauge how close we are by how densely the symbols are grouped. Once we're sure we're close, I'll use the intel our client provided to direct you to the relic. They tell me that these guys keep the thing pretty well guarded, but, despite their magic, they're still only human."

Zane cocked a brow, "Which reminds me: why am I sharing the pay with you when I could just as easily do this whole thing myself? I could be in, out, and halfway down the mountain before one of them could blink an eye, and short of a few magic tricks there's not a damn thing they can do that any other of their species can do! What are you gonna be doing?"

Raith sneered and gave his friend a punch in the shoulder, "Same as usual: keeping your ass out of trouble! You remember Paris?"

"Alright, Paris was *not* my fault!"

Raith rolled his eyes, "You tripped on your own feet and set off the damn alarms!"

Zane shook his head, "Only because you bought those piece-of-shit shoes!"

"Uh huh," Raith shook his head, "And was it the shoes' fault that the guard shot you four times?"

"In my defense, that asshole was clearly eager to pull the trigger on *anybody*!" Zane shook his head, "If I'd have been human then there's no way I'd have survived."

"Yea, I think that was sort of the point."

"Look, man, you don't have to get snippy just because I proved that you're only here to keep me from getting bored." Zane hip-checked Raith and watched as he stumbled beside a cluster of rocks, "I'd split the earnings with you either—Hey! It's one of those cliff-things!"

Raith frowned and followed Zane's gaze to the rocks and, sure enough, caught sight of a few partially faded symbols carved into them.

"They're called 'glyphs'," he corrected, glancing around for any others, "And good eye."

The two grew silent as the promise of their goal grew nearer. Continuing on, they began to spot more and more of the symbols carved into the varying-sized rocks littered about the mountaintop until they finally came to a polished portion of the ground that was littered in them. Marveling at the spectacle for a moment, they drifted into the center of the site.

"Their village must be just over that pass," Raith nodded towards a rise ahead of them, "Which means this is as far as I can go without risking being seen."

Zane nodded, sliding his backpack from his shoulders and retrieving a few of his blades. As he began to secure the weapons to his hips and left leg, he looked up at his friend, "Northern side of the mountain, right?"

Raith nodded, "Closer to the Northern side, but still occupying the center region. I've been told you'll see a large structure that's been carved into the mountain; this serves as their church. The relic should be just beyond that." He frowned at the blades, "You're not planning on using those, are you?"

"Not unless I have to," Zane shrugged before he returned the now-empty backpack to his shoulders. "But I don't take any chances ever since getting shot by a trigger-happy French security guard!"

Raith scoffed, "These guys aren't going to use guns on you, Zane."

Zane shrugged, "Acid cannons, laser pistols, or magic wands! Either way, I'm prepared."

"Magic wands don't sound too farfetched, actually," Raith laughed.

Zane smirked, "Yea, too bad I didn't bring a camera. I'm sure snapping a picture of something like that would make you die laughing. Anyway…" He gave his friend a nod, "Be back in a flash."

"Be sure you are," Raith offered.

But Zane was already gone.

Zane groaned as he was dropped on the frigid stone slab.
Where was he?
Hadn't he been…?
Light. He remembered blue light.
Like lightning.
And pain.
Had he tripped agai—
Hands began to grab and pull at him; yanking his limbs and slamming his head back into the rock he lay upon.
"H-hey! Ow! What the fuck?"
His eyes opened and the vicious glare from the sun blinded him as his senses reawakened all at once.
The scent of blood and…

And the sound of tortured cries.

"Raith? RAITH?" Zane thrashed against the binds and hands that held him against the frigid stone slab, "G-get off me! GET OFF! WHAT THE FUCK ARE YOU DOING TO HIM? RAITH? RAITH!"

The blood curdling cries of his friend were all the evidence Zane needed to know that, whatever they were doing to him, it wasn't something he'd want to see. Fully registering this, however, he couldn't bring himself to stop his struggling against his captors to see past them; to get a glimpse of what the taroe chief was doing.

It wasn't supposed to have been like this!

It was just a job!

A simple job!

It was never supposed to—

There was a pause in Raith's cries—a bitter-sweet break in the pained howls—that was occupied by a jagged and tortured hiss as Raith struggled to inhale.

~Five Minutes Earlier~

Somehow they'd known!

Somehow they'd been prepared!

It had all happened in a flash. Practically the moment Zane had vanished from Raith's sight the ground had gone electric beneath his feet. All at once his body ceased to be his, and his therion form had exploded to the surface in a single moment of bone-and-organ twisting agony. He'd never felt the change like that—his entire body growing and shifting all at once—and it had been enough to force him to his knees.

Only by the time he'd fallen he was in his human form once again.

Unable to muster enough control to move his eyes, let alone transform again.

And then they'd closed in on him…

By the time the taroe soldiers had dragged him to the center of their village, Zane was already stripped and bound to a slab of rock; his eyes swimming lazily about within his skull as he mumbled incoherently in response to the taroes' harsh treatment.

"You came here to steal from us, yes?" A deep, gravelly voice that sounded as though it was coming from the rocks themselves issued from the depths of the temple. A moment later, a tall, robust silhouette appeared at the entrance and a dark-skinned man brandishing one of Zane's blades stepped towards them. As he drew nearer, the others of the taroe tribe paused in their onslaught and half-knelt before the newcomer long enough for him to offer a nod at their gesture. No sooner had they dipped their bodies in his direction then they'd returned to their tasks. Closing the distance between him and Raith, the man—his enchanted tattoos already glowing bright enough to cut through even the daylight—brought the flat of the long blade against Raith's naked side with enough force to make him flinch. "Answer me, you wretched cur! You and that *leech* came here to steal from us, did you not? To steal *this*?"—one of the nearby taroe subjects suddenly lifted the relic into view—"*This* is why you've come?"

Raith struggled to pull away, but his weakened body was unable to shake the men that held him.

"Father?" Raith's eyes widened at the familiar voice, "Father, what's... OH MY—N-no! What's happening?"

The chief turned and motioned towards Nicc'oule—tears already streaming down her face—and several of his subject closed in and caught her before she could reach him. Knowing that she'd meet a similar—if not harsher—punishment for her involvement in their plans, Raith shook his head and silently urged her not to get herself involved.

Seeing the intent in his plea, however, only motivated her that much more.

"DON'T DO THIS! RELEASE THEM! FATHER, PLEASE—I IMPLORE YOU!—DON'T LET THIS GO ON ANY—"

"Take her away," the chief ordered. "She is young and innocent still; there is no need to corrupt her with such matters." Turning back, he nodded to the taroe who still held the relic. "Begin the preparations for the *Maledictus*!"

Overhearing this, Nicc'oule howled with sorrow and, with her tattoos glowing brighter than Raith had ever seen, began to try to fight off the guards who held her. Despite all her efforts, however, their magic proved just as effective at neutralizing her spells, and her cries of protest grew dimmer as she was dragged away.

Fighting the tears that threatened to grow in his eyes, Raith looked down, choking back the sorrowful proclamations of love he'd never got to offer her…

"YOU FUCKS! YOU SICK FUCKS! LEAVE HIM ALONE, OR I SWEAR I'LL RIP EVERY ONE OF YOUR—AHHHH!" The cold that had begun to seep into Zane's core was flooded by scorching pain. Fighting against the leather bind that held his head, he pushed to see the source.

Then suddenly wished he hadn't.

The dagger was nearly buried to the hilt; the few inches still protruding allowing him to see the rusted and serpentine metal that had been embedded in his belly.

"Silence that wretch," the chief's voice rose over the celebratory jeers of the taroe tribe. "I'll tolerate no more of his flapping tongue!"

"Shall I carve it from his head?"

Zane wretched and whimpered as the dagger was yanked from his guts and a length of intestine followed.

Raith's cries were stifled then, the chief letting out a grunt as he fought to maintain control of the therion.

"No," the chief's voice oozed with malicious intent, "he'll suffer far more if we allow him to keep his voice. Here, use these."

Zane whimpered as he felt the warmth of his insides begin to worm down his hip. "What… what do you want from us? Wh-what—"

A pair of hands seized his face and forced his lips open as another taroe leaned in and pushed two fleshy lengths into his mouth. The taste of therion blood—*Raith's* blood!—rolled over his tongue before it seeped down his throat. His vampire body ignored the bitter taste of the source and excitedly compelled Zane to seek out more, but his awareness of who the blood belonged to made him wretch. As his bound body quaked with spasms of nausea, he felt a pair of hardened points rake against his lips.

Claws...

His eyes widened and a muffled cry squeezed around the two fingers that had been cut from Raith's hand.

"I think the filthy blood-sucker *likes* it!"

"Disgusting creatures!"

"One of you help me," the chief called out. "This wretched dog won't keep his eyes open!"

As a few of Zane's captors stepped away from the blood-covered stone slab he'd been secured to, Raith's cries started up again.

"Open the vampire up! Prepare him for what's coming," the chief ordered, still grunting over his unseen work with Raith. "You there! Free the therion of his thieving heart!"

The dagger once again found its way into the depths of Zane's stomach, and the taroe wielding it began the long and purposeful process of sawing from the far side of his right hip to the left. When the process was finished, the blade was removed and embedded in his thigh to free the wielder's hands so that he could begin shoveling the bulk of Zane's insides onto his lap.

As Zane was brought to a new threshold of pain that he'd never thought possible, his mind began to warp the scene around him until all he could hear was Raith's cries of agony.

They were just as much his own now.

Zane coughed and gagged on his friend's severed fingers, struggling to keep the self-lubricating hunks of meat from sliding down his throat.

He wanted to curse.

He wanted to yell.

He wanted to say whatever it would take to get the taroe to release Raith.

It was his fault! His greed that had brought them there and his carelessness that had gotten them caught!

He'd brought ruin and death to one of the people he cared about most...

"Yes," the chief's voice rumbled over him and he shifted his gaze to take in the taroe's leering face, "you've brought ruin and death to one that you love." He paused long enough to nod to the taroe who'd just finished with Zane's insides, who wiped his hands on his chest before yanking the dagger from Zane's thigh and stepping around the stone slab to join the chief by Zane's head. "And that is only the beginning…"

The rusted, blood-stained dagger fell out of focus as its tip neared Zane's right eye, and he hissed and fought to turn his head away from the encroaching weapon.

"HOLD HIM! KEEP HIS EYES OPEN!"

"Don't think that I won't free you of your eyelids to force you to watch, vampire!"

More and more taroe hands gripped his head and pried his eyes open, and the dull, crusted metal began the slow and calculated path in carving his eye from his skull. With the right half of his vision rapidly falling into a dull, dark crimson, Zane's left eye—darting about in a chaotic panic—caught sight of a familiar brown eye, blood-soaked and dangling by its optic nerve from the delicately pinched fingers of a nearing taroe, as it was offered to the chief.

"The therion's eye, sire!"

"Excellent! Now to deliver it to its new owner!"

Whimpering around his agony and confusion, Zane felt a flood of cold air fill the vacant cavity as his mutilated right eye was tugged free of his body. Stepping aside, the taroe who had robbed him of one eye made room for the other as Raith's stolen organ was fed into the vacant orifice.

"Good… Good! Now… the heart! Bring me the therion's heart! And get the relic in place," the chief leaned in towards Zane's left side—the only side that still offered the suffering vampire any sight—and wet his lips, "You'll be pleased to know that you'll be leaving here with what you came to steal. I truly hate to part with it—we all do, actually—but the punishment you've earned demands that you be burdened with what you sought so greatly to wrong us for. May its weight add all the more to your already sizable burden, *Maledictus*!"

Zane groaned as the chief yanked Raith's fingers from his mouth, freeing him of its effects.

"Wh-what… why are you—"

"Don't you dare ask us 'why', *Maledictus*!"

Zane tried to blink—tried to focus beyond his agony to understand the word—but the stolen eye that now occupied his face made the act excruciating. "Wh-who is… M-Male…"

"*Maledictus*," the chief repeated for him, his voice suddenly gentle, "It is what you'll be known as from henceforth. Now, prepare yourself, this next part *will* hurt…"

~Three Days Later~

Zane was only distantly aware of the injuries he was sustaining as his body crashed down the side of the mountain. The sound of his bones breaking with each impact against the jagged rocks that stood between him and the base of the mountain were no more relevant than that of the branches he snapped along the fall.

All of it meant nothing.

He wasn't afraid of death; something deep within him— whether it was the wretched relic that had been crammed beneath his ribcage or the severed heart of his butchered friend that now beat beside his own—knew full-well that he wouldn't die that easily.

No.

If he'd learned anything from that weekend, it was that death was not as easily achieved as one might imagine. *Especially* when the combined magic of hundreds of malicious magic-wielding chanters refused to let it!

No…

They hadn't thrown him from that mountain to kill him.

They'd simply freed something infinitely worse than death into the world!

Nicc'oule couldn't see past the burning haze of her tear filled eyes. She hadn't been able to stop crying since the moment she'd seen Raith captured. That wretched thing *had* been cursed; it *had* been evil. Wherever it had come from—whatever its purposes—it had poisoned her entire tribe and turned them into ravenous lunatics.

It had driven them to use the one spell their people had sworn *never* to unleash.

A spell that should have never been allowed to be brought into existence.

A spell every bit as horrible as the relic that had driven it into being.

A spell called *Maledictus*...

She'd wanted only to free her people of the thing that she saw as a cancer to the goodness of her people, and her efforts had gotten the man she loved killed.

And now his friend—this vampire; this... Zane—was forced to carry the literal weight of his death beside his heart; was forced to see the world through the shared gaze of a beloved friend.

This Zane would have to carry their failure through every terrible act that the enchanted ink they'd laced beneath his flesh condemned him to commit.

And when word got out to the mythos Council that a taroe tribe had committed this unspeakable act on one of their own, there would be hell to pay.

Still unable to see past the burning haze of her tear filled eyes, she blindly navigated the chasm to her and Raith's secret cave; a cave that she'd never again get to share with him.

Soon enough her village would be wiped out—made an example of by the non-human government who had made it clear to their people long ago that the *Maledictus* curse was *never* to be anything but a rumor. And while there seemed to be a poetic justice in letting Raith's people see an end to her life for getting him mixed up in her tribe's troubles, she couldn't bring herself to stand upon the ground as one of the monsters that her people had allowed themselves to become...

Zane groaned, struggling to get his thoughts to function in a way he could decipher. Though he wasn't sure how he knew or how he'd come to be there, he was certain that he was in his bed. The familiarity and serenity of the home he'd built with Celine was unmistakable...

But something about it felt hollow and incomplete.

Forcing his body to move, he sat up—hearing his bones and joints moan and crack and protest every inch of the way—and scanned the empty bedroom for any sign of Celine. Seeing that he was, in fact, alone in the room, he forced himself to his feet and stumbled his way to the bathroom, feeling, for the first time in a long time, as though he was hung over.

The dull hum of fluorescence set a skeptical calm in his mind as he started towards the toilet, eager to empty his strained bladder. Passing by the mirror, however, a new priority presented itself.

Tattoos!

Dozens of them!

The suddenly familiar tribal designs snaked all over his arms and shoulders, littering his chest and starting up his neck!

And his eyes...

The familiar silver of Raith's therion form now occupied the right side of his face...

Then...

"Welcome to this world, Male—"

Zane howled in the sudden recollection of every second of agony he'd endured. Dropping to his knees, his bladder emptied itself and he vomited on himself.

"YOU FUCKS! YOU SICK FUCKS! LEAVE HIM ALONE, OR I SWEAR I'LL... I'll... I'll..."

His eyes widened as more memories came:

The mountain—the fall—and his broken body laying useless at the base...

His friends, the men he'd grown up with before he'd been turned...

Celine...

He'd been taken home?

He'd...

He looked at his hands and saw blood.

"No... No no no! This... this is a dream! Not real! Can't be..."

You know what we did, Zane! And while your little whore was a tasty starter, we're still feeling a little puckish.

Zane cried out and pitched around, certain he'd heard...

"Who's there?"

Silence...

"Dammit! I know you're there! Come out and—"

And WHAT, limp-dick! You gonna start some shit with the likes of us? Cinch up your leaky cunt and put your balls where they belong, you sniveling fucking shit! There's fun to be had, and we're not gonna wipe baby-boy's ass while he comes to cope!

"Wh-where's Celine? Who are yo—"

WE'RE YOU, BITCH! AND YOU'RE US! AND UNTIL WE SQUAT OUT A FRESH SHIT ON WHATEVER OPEN WOUND WE INFLICT IN THE NEXT HOUR, CELINE'S IN HERE WITH US, TOO! NOW GET OUT THERE AND FIND US SOME FUCKING PAIN OR WE'LL BRING OUR OWN RIGHT HERE; RIGHT NOW!!

No sooner had the threat been uttered than Zane's body was alive with every ounce of pain the taroe had inflicted on him! His howls of pain shook through ever atom of his body and his right eye ached as his field of vision shifted and warped...

And then he saw the blood-red aura fade into being around him.

"B-but... that can't be..."

Previous encounters with auric vampires—the mind feeders of their kind—had made it clear that the unseen energy around his body registered as blue...

Blue!

Red was the color of...

"R-Raith?"

Not anymore, sweetheart!

CHAPTER TEN
THE GHOST OF YOU

THE CHILLED FALL WINDS WRAPPED around Serena as she walked through the city.

There was so much on her mind.

Too much on her mind!

After that night, she'd been forcing herself to stay awake in hope of another visit-slash-vision with Zane; anything that might bring with it any sort of lead to where he might be. After several disappointing nights of ongoing loneliness, however, she'd given up on a repeat performance.

But then, that last night, he'd come to her again.

There were no words—none that she could hear, at least—and the peaceful pale light and calm, loving demeanor had been replaced by a tortured, blood-bathed specter who's silent cries haunted her room for less than five minutes before his ghost had finally exploded out of existence and left her screaming his name and crying in the middle of her floor.

Zoey had nearly had to put her in an auric-induced coma just to calm her down, and when she'd finally awoken nearly fourteen hours later she was bogged by a feeling that she'd fought for so long to escape.

Fear.

As the thoughts wrapped her into her own cocoon of solitude, she sensed a strangely familiar auric signature and turned in time to see a shadowed figure crawling up the side of a building. Shaking herself out of her own thoughts, she hurried to follow after them, taking care not to arouse suspicion in the crowded city streets, and keeping her aura out to scan the area in hopes of figuring out who it was.

Finally slipping free of the crowded streets and ducking into an alley—*Why is it always an alley?* She rolled her eyes—calling upon her recently discovered parkour skill set to carry her to the rooftop and spotted Axle crouching on a ledge, a backpack filled to bulging capacity strapped to his shoulders, before leaping to the next rooftop

She frowned at the sight, noticing that both his movements and his aura weren't what she'd come to expect from him. Scowling at this, she put up an auric shield to mask her scent and any sounds she might make before starting after him, eager to see what it is he was up to.

Though his style seemed more clunky than before—his movement driven by powerful leaps and hardened sprints rather than the previously agility-focused run they'd shared before—there was no mistaking his personal grace as she follow him from building to building until they'd reached the business district.

Where was he going? This wasn't the way to the orphanage…

And where were the others of his group? If this had something to do with a job, wouldn't they have been with him?

She continued to follow, feeling more concerned than ever.

Where could he be going?

Landing on the rooftop of the new clan's headquarters, Axle stumbled and paused to catch his breath.

Seeing her chance, Serena dropped down with him, dropping her shields and using the tucked roll she'd learned from him.

"We going to make this place our thing or something?" She chuckled, starting towards him, "What the hell are you doing, anyway?"

Startled, Axle jumped to face his sudden company, dropping his bag and frowning as he saw her.

"Ser... Serena?" He blinked, his aura coiling tightly over his head before suddenly relaxing and beginning a slow sway over his head. "What are you...?"

"That's what I'm asking you, bud," Serena let her voice soften as she stepped forward, "Axle, what's wrong? You're acting funny."

"I-I don't know," He shook his head suddenly. "Isn't this..."—he looked down at the bag and bit his lip—"Isn't this what I normally do?"

His eyes seemed so lost...

"Where are the others?" Serena bit her lip as she watched him.

"Huh? Others?"

Serena nodded slowly, "Yea. You know, your gang? Your *friends*?"

"I... I don't know," he held his head, frowning. "I couldn't find them after I woke up. I just thought..." More blinking.

"What?" Serena pressed, "What did you think?"

"I... didn't." He looked up, looking nervous, "I didn't think anything of it. I just..." He looked down at the backpack, "Isn't this what I normally do?"

His aura tightened into a coil again and bobbed angrily over his head. Groaning, he blinked against what Serena could only guess was the worst headache he'd ever had and finally took a step towards her. Something HAD happened to him and she was more concerned than before as she stepped towards him.

"Axle, you should come with me," she placed her hand on his shoulder and he jumped a bit at the contact before taking a deep breath and turning to face her.

"Where?" Axle frowned, biting his lip, "Where would you take me? Your clan *is* after me..."

"Well, you're coming with me anyway," Serena smiled warmly. "It's going to be safer for you anyway."

"Safer... A-are you sure?" He shook his head, looking slightly dazed as he took a deep breath again.

"Sure I'm sure. Now come on, man; you look like alv shit," Serena frowned.

"Thanks... I guess." He blushed at her comment.

"Hey? You like bikes?" Serena smirked.

"What?" He blinked.

Serena rolled her eyes, "Come on, doofus."

The two of them made their way off the rooftop, heading back towards where Serena had first spotted him and returning to where she'd parked her motorcycle.

"Is this yours?" Axle blushed, turning to her and smirking slightly, "Why am I not surprised?"

"Oh my... is that a glimmer of your trademark wit?" Serena teased, "Careful with that; the dead-eyed doofus police might come and get you. Now get on."

Her playful banter seemed to break past some of the haze that had crippled him earlier, and he smiled as he looked back at the bike and ran his hand across the electric-purple paint job. "It suits you," he smiled slightly, "beautiful and streamlined, but deadly."

Serena blushed and quickly moved to the bike, straddling it and starting it up as she turned to him. "Flattery only gets you halfway there! Now," she smirked once more at him as she moved forward in the seat. "Hop on!"

Axle nodded and climbed on behind her.

"Make sure you secure your backpack," Serena called over her shoulder. "We don't need a bunch of Benjamins littering the street. That's a good way to get bad attention."

Axle's aura tightened again. "Backpack?"

"Yea. Remember? That bloated thing *filled* with money that you were—tell me you didn't leave it on the damn roof!" Serena groaned.

Axle blushed and started stammering.

"Whatever. Don't even worry about it," Serena shook her head as she started off down the road. "Happy night for those assholes, I guess."

"Sorry..." Axle finally offered, securing himself by wrapping his arms around her waist.

Feeling a flood of warmth from the contact a familiar feeling fluttered in her lower belly, Serena bit her lip against a wave of guilt and forced herself to shake the partially-formed thoughts in her head from existence. "No worries," she shrugged, "You can just work it off as my personal slave. So did you get lost back there? The orphanage is *East* from here, remember?"

"The orphanage..." Axle's aura flared with recollection, "I

guess I just got a little turned around. I... I mean, I think I actually *forgot* where I was taking it..." Another auric shift returned him to the tightened coil, "What's wrong with me?"

"I'm not sure," Serena admitted over her shoulder, "But I am going to get to the bottom of it all once we're back at the Vail Clan!"

Axle's arms tightened around her waist, and another flood of heat struck her as she felt his lean-yet-muscled body press against her back.

"Thanks again for helping me, Serena," Axle said as they stepped off the motorcycle after she parked it at the clan's headquarters. "If you hadn't showed up when you did, I'm not sure where I might have ended up."

"Don't mention it." Serena looked over, "And I mean that *literally*! My colleagues here are going to have enough trust issues with you *without* you going on about how I found you running around downtown aimlessly lost in la-la land with who-knows-how-much cash. *That* nugget of information stays between us, *capisce*?"

Axle nodded.

They headed inside the clan and Serena frowned as Zoey hurried over to the two of them, shaking her head more and more viciously with each step.

"Are you out of your mind, Serena? I mean, have you *legitimately* lost it? What is *he* doing here?" She frowned, "He's not exactly on The Council's good side, and *him* walking around freely *here* is a very, very fast way to put *us* in equally bad standings!"

"Zoey, this is a matter of that trust thing we talked about. He's staying here, and I need you to keep that *quiet* around the others. He doesn't know where the rest of his gang is and something is up with his head." Serena frowned, "Please, Zoey, I need you to help me with this."

Zoey sighed, "Well, about that..."

Serena frowned, "I don't like that tone. What is it now?"

"One of our warriors found one of his gang member's behind

a casino." She shook her head, "It wasn't a pretty sight, either. The body had been mutilated."

"What?" Axle frowned, his body beginning to shake with rage, "Who would do that?"

"Calm down! Even you admitted that it was weird that they were missing, there's no point in going batshit about what you must have suspected now," Serena frowned. "Well that settles it, Zoe; something is *definitely* going on here. I don't care what the new clan's methods might be, leaving butchered mythos bodies—rogue criminals or not—in potential sight of human onlookers is *not* how things are done. Has The Council been notified about this?"

"Of course," Zoey nodded.

Serena smirked, "Did you throw the newbies under the bus to them?"

Zoey smirked, "I might've mentioned their 'incompetence' and 'irresponsibility' in passing."

Serena smirked, "Girl, I could *kiss* you! Good job! Now, as for this lug here," she nodded towards Axle, "somebody's been doing some *serious* tinkering in his head. If we keep him here then we can be sure that he'll be safe from whoever did this. Pardon my paranoia, but I don't think our new allies in that other clan are as clean as The Council would like to believe."

Zoey frowned, "Do you realize that in all my years as a warrior with the Vail Clan I've *never* gone against a single authority figure? Then you take up the role as leader and in only a few short months I'm impaling Council members with parking meters and engaged in conspiracy theories about a group that, on any other day, we *should* be thanking for their support."

Serena smirked, "Quit'cha bitching, Zoey! You know you like being a bad girl—I've got about fifteen inches worth of proof on my side, too—and you *know* your ass *loves* me for letting you free your naughty side like this."

Rolling her eyes, Zoey turned to face Axle, "I'm sorry for your loss. And I sincerely hope—for your sake—that Serena's right about you," she offered a sly grin. "I wasn't joking about the parking meter; just something to keep in mind if you're thinking of trying something."

Serena smirked, "Oh man, it was awesome! Like something straight out of a comic book; full-on X-Men's Magneto style! *Bam gurgle gurle gaahh!*"

Axle and Zoey stared at her.

"You had sugar again, didn't you?" Zoey sighed.

"I might've bought a Snickers bar while I was out," Serena stuck her tongue out.

Zoey sighed, "A whole Snickers bar. We're all doomed…"

"Hey," Serena frowned, "What's that supposed to mean?"

"You have to ask?" Zoey raised an eyebrow, "'*Bam gurgle gurle gaahh*'," she chuckled, "A full-grown kid hyped-up from *that* much processed sugar with the strength of a trained sang warrior *and* the sort of auric control that could allow one to castrate a mouse from one-hundred meters away? Yea, I'd say we're doomed!"

"Ooh… castrating a mouse from a hundred meters away?" Serena pursed her lips.

"Crap," Zoey shook her head, "Now I'm giving her ideas." She glanced back at Axle, "Good luck."

"Th-thank you," Axle called out after her. Looking back at Serena he smiled, "She seems nice."

Serena nodded, "Yup. She's my bestie. Just don't get any ideas about her; she's already got one mutant member to deal with."

"Huh?"

"Nevermind. Follow me."

"Thanks again, Serena." Axle sighed as he followed down the clan's halls with her.

"Will you stop *thanking* everybody? Jeez! You're making everything seem so… I don't know, thank-worthy or whatever," Serena frowned and turned to him once more.

Axle smirked suddenly, his aura shifting over his head. "So much for those shining finishing school grades, eh princess?"

Serena blinked. "What did you just say?"

Another shift—the aura withdrawing into its tight coil once again—and the nervous, lost gaze returning after several blinks. "I…" He frowned, mouthing the words to himself again, "I don't know where that came from…"

Serena stared at him in disbelief. There was *definitely* something different about him, but it wasn't just that that was bothering her.

No, it wasn't that at all.

It was the new sense of familiarity she felt around him suddenly that sparked her sudden worry and interest all at once.

Sighing, she led him to a spare room that neighbored her own and smiled. "If you need anything, my room is two doors down and on the right hall. So… uh, yea! Goodnight and all."

He nodded and headed into the room. Even from down the hall, she could hear his gasp of awe at the luxurious furnishings. Chuckling, she stepped inside her own room and slipped out of her top to get ready for bed. Drawing nearer to Zane's prized mattress, however, the effort of retrieving a new shirt became a near-impossible burden and she allowed herself to fall into bed, using the last of her energy to shimmy out of her pants and crawl under the covers.

At least things were starting to get interesting…

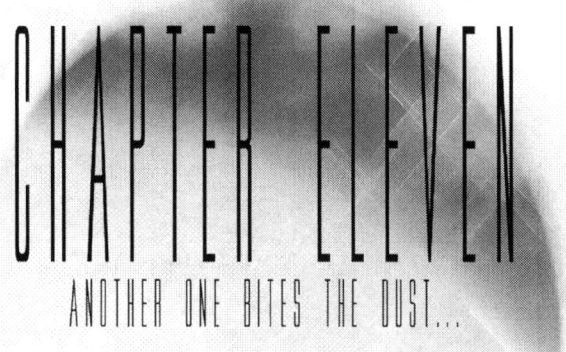

CHAPTER ELEVEN
ANOTHER ONE BITES THE DUST...

"*SERENA...*" ZANE'S VOICE WHISPERED. "*Wake up, Serena...*"

Serena jolted to a start as she was met with only her dark empty bedroom. Sighing, she let her face fall into her hands and she felt the fear growing through her body.

Zane...

"Please! Where are you?" She sobbed, "I... I can't. C'mon, Serena! Time to get a grip!" She dragged herself out of bed and started the water in her shower.

Stepping under the near-scalding water and feeling it cascade down her body, she let out a sigh and willed her tension to drip off of her with the beads of moisture. Finally, after simply standing under the stream of water until she'd mustered enough willpower to finally turn it off, she stepped out and wiped the fog from her mirror so she could look at the face waiting in her clouded reflection. Her purple eyes had dark circles under them, and her platinum-blonde hair was long overdue for a trip to the salon.

"Shit... I look like a hippie's stock broker..." She sneered and turned away from her reflection.

After a quick pass with a towel, she threw a pair of jeans and a black tank-top over her still-damp skin before she stepped out of the bathroom and right into Axle's chest.

Gasping at the unsuspected guest, she looked up at him, locking her exhausted gaze on his own and...

Driving the palm of her right hand into his nose.

"What the fu—What was that for?" Axle garbled behind the hand that was slowing the blood-flow from his nostrils.

"Sorry, reflex," Serena shrugged, stepping past him and continuing to dry her hair. "You could've been a burglar for all I knew."

"A burg—a goddam *burglar*? This is *your* clan's headquarters! We're hidden underground in the goddam woods!"

"Goddam right," Serena shrugged, "Forest burglars are not a force to be underestimated. Maybe next time you'll reconsider moseying into my room uninvited. You realize I was *naked* in bed about twenty minutes ago! What if you'd just *moseyed* in on that?"

Axle glared at her, "If you'd have asked me about thirty seconds ago I might have said that'd been a pleasant surprise. Unfortunately getting *punched* has a bit of a stunt on my libido."

"Good to know," Serena sat on her bed. "So did you need something?"

"I thought we could chat for a bit," he frowned, biting his lip as he finished mopping up his bloody nose with tissue. Looking back at her, Serena bit her lip as she saw a flash of desire in his eyes.

She obviously hadn't punched him hard enough.

That kind desire could be a very dangerous thing for both of them...

Everything okay in there? Zoey's psychic voice rang in Serena's head, *I saw Axle go into your room and heard you scream. Did he attack you?*

Serena chuckled. *Everything's fine, Zoe; that wasn't my scream.* There was a long pause and, off in the distance, Serena sensed the exuberant roll of Zoey's aura that she recognized as her friend's laughter. *I'll be okay. Thanks for checking in.*

Severing the psychic connection with Zoey, she nodded to

Axle. "Okay," she forced herself to look away, making a few passes along the back of her already-dry neck with the towel to create an excuse, "so you wanna chat? Then chat."

"Zoey, you alright?"

Zoey frowned as she looked over at Isaac, who was staring at her. Realizing she'd been spacing out after her "talk" with Serena, she bit her lip.

"Sorry about that. I'm fine, really. Just worried about Serena, I guess." Zoey sighed as she pressed against him and he held her tighter to him. "She's been different after Zane, that's for sure. But I'm afraid of what all this stress is doing to her."

"I think you know Serena better than that," Isaac offered. "The clan will be fine, and she will be too. She always figures it out. It's always in her own reckless, vulgar way, but at least she gets results. Don't worry so much and just be there to support her like you always have."

"Isaac... you always know just the right words to say," she smiled up at him.

Isaac smirked, "Yea, every now and again I get some blood to flow to my brain."

Zoey rolled her eyes, "That was another erection joke, wasn't it?"

Isaac nodded, "I guess Serena has her impact on all of us."

"I guess so," Zoey smiled.

"What's up, Axle?" Serena frowned as she sat on the bed and watched as he paced around the room.

"I just... it feels like there's more that I need to remember!" He shook his head, biting his lip, "Like there's a safe in my brain with all this information that's just *screaming* at me to free it, but I don't know the combination."

Serena chuckled, "A thief using a safe metaphor, that's cute."

Axle paused and smirked, "There's no such thing as a *safe* metaphor."

"And a layaway into a pun!" Serena laughed. Then, "Wait..." She looked up at him, "Since when are you an intellectual joker?"

Axle blinked. "Shit," he groaned, sitting on the bed, "See what I mean?"

"Don't stress over it," Serena frowned and joined him at his side, smiling reassuringly. "If it's important enough, it will come back to you."

"It's just that..."

Serena looked over, "Hmm?"

Axle frowned, "Whenever I'm with you—whenever I'm *near* you now—I feel as if it could come back. It's then—moments like right *now*—that the voice inside the safe calls to me the loudest." He shook his head and sighed. "But, I can never fully understand what it's trying to say and all I end up with is a headache."

Serena frowned and stepped closer to him and pressed her right hand to his shoulder and began to send positive energy into him and smiled as he began to relax.

"It'll be okay. We'll figure things out." She shook her head, "Things have been tough for everyone and I know right now it *is* harder to see the light at the end of the tunnel, but it is there."

"You never struck me as the type to be a motivational speaker," he looked over.

"Yeah, I know." She laughed. "A lot has changed that's for sure! Before all this I just lived in my ex-boyfriend's cabin and hid from all responsibilities. Until one night..." She bit her lip.

"What happened that night?" He looked at her, interest growing in his eyes.

"A stranger from my dad's clan—this clan—came to find me. I kicked his ass and wound up sleeping with him," she sighed. "It's sort of a long story—one that I haven't even finished dealing with—but the moral is that I learned that things happen and you can either hide from them or bury your foot up their asses. I have my father's clan; I'm their leader now. It's my responsibility to take care of them." She shook her head, "I decided a while back that I was done hiding; now, if there's a problem, I just skull-fuck the shit out of whatever's wrong until things are right again."

"Wow. That's quite a story," Axle smirked. "So you've always been a bitch?"

"Pretty much," she smirked, "but I'm a bitch who can back it up!"

"I bet you can!" He smirked.

"That's not what I meant, perv!"

Axle chuckled, "Not what I meant either, double-perv."

"What I'm trying to say though, Axle, is that you can't give up just because the answers don't come right away," she shook her head, "Sometimes you just gotta take a hot shower and break a hunk's nose."

Axle looked over, "I'm a hunk now?"

"Did I say that out loud?"

Axle smirked and shook his head, "Nope," he looked down, "Thank you for the—"

"So help me, Axle," Serena held up a finger, "if you thank me even one more goddam time I am going break more than just your nose tonight."

Axle nodded, getting up. "That's fair, I guess," leaning over, he kissed her cheek and started out. Pausing at the door, he turned and smiled, "But thanks."

"Son of a bitch!" Serena jumped to her feet to charge at him, laughing as she brandished her pillow as a weapon.

But Axle had already slammed the door to run off, the sound of his own laughter growing distant before the door to his own room blocked out his cackles.

Tossing the pillow back on the bed, Serena paused to touch her hand to the electric warmth that lingered on her cheek. Before her mind had a chance to gain any momentum she shook her head, "Stop it, Serena. Grip! Time to get a grip!"

Throwing on her boots, she stepped out of the room and headed to the garage.

She was *aching* to relieve some tension on her bike.

And she had the *perfect* destination in mind!

Serena's started forcing the automatic doors open before she'd even reached the top of the steps and, by the time she'd reached them, they'd been broken from the strain on the motor.

"Oops! Yo, bitch, your boss in *yet?*"

"Oh, it's you," the secretary sneered.

"Damn right, it's *me*! Now, where's your boss?" Serena glared.

Once again, the secretary looked down at the computer for less than a second before looking back up at her and smirking. "I'm afraid they're, like, not in at the moment. Can I take a—"

"Look, Crayola-cunt, I've had enough of you. You speak like you look—broken and painfully dull despite an ongoing effort to appear bright—and I don't think you could convey a message from me if there was a whole collection of clown makeup offered up as a prize!" Serena glared, "Now you're going to tell me *exactly* what's going on here, or I'm going to throw your broken carcass down the fucking freight elevator and piss down the shaft on whatever's left twitching!"

"Ma'am, if you don't, like, totally calm down I *will* call security."

"Let me make this crystal-fucking-clear: I am the *leader* of the Vail Clan—I have dispatched, dismembered, and then *forgotten* far greater forces than you *or* your monster-dick security guards—and if you even *try* to have me thrown out those doors again, I will deal with *all* of you, have my words with your leader, and then I will leave wearing a brand new fucking outfit with your *eyeballs* as my new favorite earrings! Now, are you going to tell me what I want to know or do I need to get *really* nasty up in this shit-hole?"

The secretary pressed the security call button.

"You stupid little bitch."

"Is there going to be a problem here?" One of the guards glared, "Might we remind you that *any* unwelcome interference with a clan leader's business is considered an act against The Council?"

Serena sneered and nodded, "Yes… that's right. Wouldn't want to interrupt your boss's very important business. Okay," she held out her arms, "take me away officers! Second verse; same as the first, right?

The three guards growled and closed in to escort Serena out.

Shaking her head, Serena forked out her purple aura and snared the two outer guards a split-second before bringing them together with enough force to slam their skulls together and knock them out. Seeing his comrades collapse in front of him, the third gawked—unsure of what had happened—before finally glaring at Serena and drawing a modified Taser.

"You know how to use that toy?" Serena chuckled.

She'd seen this particular piece of "less lethal" device in action. Along with the typical electric shock—albeit a far greater voltage than anything the humans had ever seen—the barbs were enchanted with a set of spells designed to temporarily render any species of non-human completely immobile for several hours.

There was, however, a rather unsettling side effect.

The guard growled, "I'm positive I'll manage."

As his fingers tightened on the trigger, Serena jumped into overdrive. Her muscles and eyes shifted—pushed to the next level of movement and perception by her sangsuigan body—and she watched as the room slowed to a time-frozen crawl. Moving towards the guards at a speed that they wouldn't even register as a blur, Serena retrieved two sticks of the secretary's bubblegum from her desk. From there, she stepped in front of the mid-firing Taser and, using the gum as a barrier to protect her fingers from the electric current, gripped the two barbs and jammed them into the time-frozen security therion's shoulder; a momentary flash of electric and magical discharge flaring and the body slowly twitching under the flood of energy.

Repositioning herself in front of the secretary's desk, Serena made a note of breaking both of the obnoxious sang's index fingers and wedging the piece of gum she was in the middle of chewing in her hair before finally dropping out of overdrive.

The room came alive with the pained howls of the guard as his body was thrown into spasms and he collapsed to the floor and the secretary shrieked at the sudden flood of pain coming from both hands.

"So glad we could have this little chat, darling," Serena smiled at the secretary. "Your friends there"—she motioned to the three hulking therions that were sprawled in the middle of the floor—"made a good point: it's not right to interrupt a clan leader when they're conducting business." She shrugged, "Now *this* clan leader *will* be returning in the *very*-near future to conduct her own business, and I suggest you all remember what we've learned today and *not* interrupt. Now, you're going to have a mess with that one"—she pointed to the Tasered therion—"in about ten seconds when his system voids its bowels, so I hope you have a janitor on call, as well." Turning, she walked towards the door with an added swagger before pausing, "Oh... and you've got something in your hair." Smirking, she raised her hand to wave, "Like, bye... and junk!"

Serena turned away paused when the automatic doors wouldn't open and she sighed, throwing out her aura and blowing the glass out before stepping through.

"And your door's broken too."

Making her way towards her bike, she frowned as she began to wonder more about what the clan was up to that warranted such secrecy from one of their own.

The whole thing just stank of conspiracy.

As she returned to the alley where she'd parked her bike, she frowned at the familiar scent of fresh blood and spotted she saw a leg jutting out from a pile of trash. Frowning, she stepped over and, kicking a few of the topmost garbage bags out of the way, uncovered two more of Axle's friends. Just like Zoey had described of the first one, the two bodies were horribly mutilated; most of their skin having been torn off completely or left in shredded ribbons. All over each of them were the unmistakable tracks of claws and teeth, though not like the kind that Serena was used to seeing from therion attacks.

Cursing under her breath, she pulled out her phone and dialed Zoey's direct line.

"Serena? What's up?" Zoey's voice already sounded worried.

"I found two more of Axle's friends," Serena informed her. "Same situation as the first."

"Oh my..." Zoey sighed, "How bad are they?"

"It looks like they were a main course in some twisted buffet for *something*," Serena sneered, "Doesn't look like anything we've dealt with before. Completely different calling card if you ask— hold on." Serena narrowed her eyes at something that glistened under the beam from a streetlight behind her. I hadn't been until she'd shifted her body and allowed the light to flood over her shoulder that the small something caught her attention.

"Serena?" Zoey's voice called out through her phone, "What is it?"

Serena looked at the small object for a moment before finally bringing it to her nostrils and sniffing it.

"Oh shit," she gagged.

"What? What is it? Serena?"

"It's fine, Zoey. It's…" Serena sneered and tossed the clue to the ground, shaking her hand in disgust once it was free of the clue, "It's a giant scale."

"A what?"

"A scale! Like from a giant-ass snake or something! Thing smells like an iguana's taint!"

"Do I want to know how you'd know—"

"It was a joke, Zoey! Can you just send a cleanup crew? Maybe somebody who might know what we're dealing with."

"Okay, Serena. I'll forward the cleanup crew the location on your cell phone's GPS. See you soon."

With that, the two hung up and Serena hopped on her bike and headed back towards the clan, making it there in only half her normal time.

Heading inside, she was greeted by Zoey, Isaac, Nikki and Raith.

"Where's Axle?"

"He wanted to be alone after I told him the news," Zoey bit her lip.

"That's fine for now," Serena sighed and looked back to Zoey, "Any word from the brains what could've done this?"

"There was, but you're not going to like it." Zoey frowned.

"Of course I'm not going to like it," Serena shook her head, "With the exception of oiled-up, psychopathic Scotsmen with a taste for mythos flesh, I doubt this is something I'm going to be taking immediate interest in enjoying the company of. Now what are we dealing with?"

"Everything you told me points to ykali."

Serena shook her head, "No, that can't be right. Those things are almost *extinct*; they'd never do something like this and call attention to themselves."

"You said it yourself, Serena: what else could it be if *not* the ykali?" Serena shrugged.

"You're asking me to believe that a six-foot lizard-man just went 'what the hell! I've had a good run on this planet, right? How 'bout we just waddle our scaly, big-clawed, sharp toothed—fuck me sideways there really is an ykali in my city," Serena buried her face in her hands. "I swear to fuck it's like the goddam plagues of Egypt are targeting my sweet blonde ass!"

Zoey frowned, "It gets worse…"

Serena kept her face cupped in her palms. "Of course it does."

"They think there's more than one."

"Oh fuck. So we have a whole *pack* of those things hunting in our streets?"

"That's the weird part. The only attacks we're getting word of are with the found bodies of Axle's gang. There has been *no* other sightings or attacks." Zoey sighed.

"Well, we'll just keep our eyes open for anymore attacks and hopefully we can even capture one to study it," Nikki offered, looking over at Raith who had begun to itch his arms suddenly as he bit his lip.

"You alright there, Raith?" Serena frowned, noticing as well.

"Yeah, I'm fine. I think I'm going to call it an early night, though. I suddenly don't feel so good," he frowned, his voice coming out deeper as he headed to his room.

"Do you want to go check on him, Nikki?" Serena frowned.

"I think he needs to be alone for some reason…" Nikki frowned more, biting her lip.

Serena frowned, nodding after a moment and smiled softly at Nikki, "We'll check on him later."

"For now, we have to worry about finding the source of these attacks and what they want with Axle's gang," Zoey sighed, shaking her head."

Agreed," Serena looked over at Nikki and the others. "I guess I'll go talk with Axle then."

CHAPTER TWELVE
LOSING HIS MIND

"AXLE?" SERENA CALLED AS SHE knocked on his door.

After a moment of no answer, she reached past the door with her aura and unlocked it from the other side before letting herself in, finding Axle crouched on the floor, clutching his head in pain.

"Axle! What happened to you?" She cried out as she kneeled over by him.

"It hurts…" He shook his head and looked over at her, the pain stretching through his face, "My head hurts so bad!"

"It's alright now…" Serena placed her right hand on the side of his face to send healing energies while cupping her left hand on his shoulder, drawing in the bulk of his pain and panic. "It's okay now." Then, smiling, "How would you like to go for a run?"

"A run?" He looked up at her.

"Yea. The forest here has some amazing trails," she smiled. "A little fresh air and exercise is always good for the head, right?"

He smiled and nodded, "That's true."

She smirked, taking his hand and leading him outside and into the thickness of the forest that surrounded their clan's headquarters.

Then, without even a warning, Serena rushed off ahead of him.

"Hey! Wait!" Axle called, starting after her, "No fair!"

"All's fair in forest-runs and warfare, slowpoke!" She called out as she laughed, jumping up onto the branch of a tree that hovered over the trail.

Waiting, she kept an eye on the trail below her and, as Axle passed by beneath her she smirked, putting up an auric shield to hide herself, and dropped down behind him.

"HOLY SHIT A MOOSE!" She cried out right as she let her shields drop.

"Wha?" Axle howled in surprise and jumped almost high enough to hit his head on the tree branch, turning towards her and smirked. "You'll pay for that."

Serena, laughing too hard to hear the threat, had to steady herself against the tree to keep from collapsing.

"Oh it is *on*!" Axle smirked.

Serena raised an eyebrow, "Is it?" She jumped into overdrive and appeared behind him, "I'm afraid that'd mean you could *catch* me," she mocked before turning and sprinting down the trail.

Axle, expecting this, started off after her, still chuckling at her prank, and soon had caught up and started a steady pace beside her as they ran through the forest.

Making their way along the path that fed out into a wider clearing that was typically used as a camp site in the summer season, Serena stopped.

"I'm really sorry about your gang…" She sighed, looking over her shoulder at him, "I know all of this must be really tough."

"It's alright," he sighed and shook his head, "Well, no. It's *not* okay; it's pretty far from okay. But it's not your fault, and I know that they wouldn't have liked the idea of me being upset over their deaths." He looked over, "It's the same way I'd feel about knowing they were suffering over me."

"That's a good way to look at it, I guess," she smiled softly and turned to the small fishing pond that bordered the camp site.

"I've been having these really weird dreams…" Axle finally

said, "Nothing clear, but I think there's something in them that might offer some answers." He sighed, sitting on a nearby log that was next to her. "I'm hoping that it may be able to tell me what I'm trying to remember so desperately."

Serena blushed and sat down beside him, "What sort of dreams are they?"

"Nothing clear enough to describe yet," he sighed and shook his head, "Just flashes of emotions and voices and sometimes colors, but they've been getting more vivid."

Serena smiled and nodded, "Well, keep me posted on them, okay?" She stood up, "Feeling better?"

He nodded.

"Good," she held out her hand to help him up, "Come on. I'm famished, and that must mean you are too. Let's head back and get some grub."

If there had ever been any doubt to Axle's species or the degree of starvation that his lifestyle up until that point had been, the degree of his consumption more than cleared the air. Though Serena was certain that the clan's pantry was stocked for well over the next couple of years, there were periods in his ravenous consumption and immediate return to refill his plate that made her wonder if they'd have enough to sate the onslaught. Finally, however—issuing a triumphant belch and letting his head fall back—he announced that he was, in fact, full and ready to get some sleep.

Still smiling from the spectacle she'd witnessed, Serena escorted him back to his room, eager to get to her own, as well. As they reached his door, Serena stopped and smiled. "You promise you're feeling better?"

He smiled, "I promise. Thanks for—"

"Don't you say it!" Serena playfully scolded, "And don't you go kissing me on the cheek again."

Blushing, Axle nodded, offering a solemn "I won't," that convinced Serena it was safe to start towards her own room.

Before she could turn away, however, his arms were around

her and pulling her against his chest as he pressed his lips to hers.

The kiss was gentle at first, almost testing her reaction. Gentle, yet filled with an emotion Serena hadn't felt in so long. When the gesture earned no response to sway him, the kiss deepened.

Serena gasped as his lips melded harder with hers; his passion came out and she lost herself in the kiss as she wrapped her arms tightly around his neck to bring him closer to her.

The warmth.

The desire.

The need for this.

It was too much.

Too much...

She was getting lost in Axle's embrace, filled with fear and longing as she desperately clawed at her core to find the strength to resist the urge to go on.

However, at that moment Axle did that just for her; abruptly, pulling away as he held his head and groaned in pain before stepping into his room. "I-I'm sorry! I need to get some rest..." He growled out before shutting the door in Serena's face.

Serena frowned, biting her lip as she glanced once more at the door and allowed the guilt to consume her as she ran for her room.

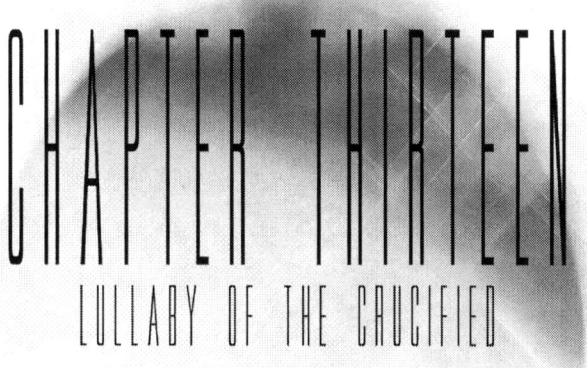

CHAPTER THIRTEEN
LULLABY OF THE CRUCIFIED

SERENA, CLOSE YOUR EYES; I'LL BE your lover tonight.

Axle blinked at the words that echoed all around him, unable to fully grasp their meaning. The pain in his head had spread and become a misery that consumed his entire being.

A misery that now seemed to taunt and condemn him.

A misery that seeped like a dense, pale fog from deep within his chest until he was surrounded in the cold, bitter clouds of his own despair. He whimpered, feeling the powerful self-loathing come down on him, forcing him to gasp against the weight of his own hatred; a hatred that turned the air in his lungs to ice.

Serena, close your eyes...

Just outside the ghostly wisps of fog were the dark phantoms of leafless trees that slowly began to define a forest that he suddenly found himself surrounded in. All at once it became clear that he was trapped there; condemned to the frigid, barren forest of his own condemnation.

"Hello?" Axle spun around in a frantic attempt to spot the source of the words that seemed to carry on the very fog itself, "Who's there?"

I'll be your lover tonight.

"WHO'S THERE, GOD DAMMIT!!"
Out of the corner of his vision, he spotted eyes—a pair of mismatched orbs that followed his every movement—and he spun to face them. But he found himself face-to-face with only one of the dark, dead trees.

Serena...

Spinning around again, he caught sight of the eyes again, this time several pairs that scattered across the landscape in his peripheral vision. Every time he turned his head to face them head-on, however, he saw only trees.
Silver and blue.
Silver and blue.
Silver and blue...
No matter where he turned the damned eyes watched him just out of his focus.
There was no escaping them!
Growling in agitation, Axle turned away—starting towards a direction that in no way differed from any other—and hoped that it would take him somewhere; anywhere! But for every step he took, his setting didn't change; the scenery didn't move.
And the eyes didn't stop staring!
Snarling, Axle forced his body to transform, feeling that he might find some comfort—some sense of safety—in his therion body. The pain of the change flooded his system as his body pitched and tossed, and he relished in every excruciating moment, knowing just how much stronger and faster he'd be when he ridded himself of...
His human body!
Looking down at his hands, he was rewarded with nothing but the sight of his weak, pink human hands. The only thing that held was the ache, which clung to his body like a freezing, mocking cancer.
He could try to run...

Buddy, what's the point!

Axle spun, growling and swiping his fists at empty air. "SHOW YOURSELF!!"

I may never know why I let you go...

Axle whimpered, fear sinking into his heart as he drew back, "Please... leave me alone—"

I'm sick of waiting!

The ground shook with violent tremors that seemed to extend into Axle's own mind—every quake causing him to tremble like a child; every distant sound of destruction seeming to fracture a part of himself. The chaos drew nearer, the trees that had stood proudly over him and held him captive succumbing to the pitching of their soil and beginning to collapse with thunderous roars that reverberated behind Axle's eyes. As the tremors continued, the ground beneath his feet began to split into violent, spider-webbed cracks—bright, blood-red light pouring from the cracks and casting a visceral haze over the forest—that began to collapse into the crimson oblivion below.

I'M SICK OF WAITING!

"Please! What have I done to—"

The lonely plot of land that Axle stood upon began to crumble, and he howled in panic as his only foothold vanished. Desperation sinking in, he hurled himself towards the nearest tree and grasped onto the upturned roots that had presented themselves in their fall. Scrambling to keep his grip he found the roots too slick to hold, and as he looked at the mass within his bone-white fist he saw that he was trying to hold himself from strands of platinum-blonde hair.

I may never know why I let you go. Serena, close your eyes...

"NO!!"

I'll be your lover tonight.

"NOOO!!"
Losing his hold, Axle plummeted into the depths of the crimson abyss. As

the void grew all-consuming, he felt himself swallowed in its sticky warmth, and with every drop that rolled across his skin he felt new levels of pain—heard new decibels of screams and wails—and saw the mismatched silver and blue eyes looming over him in the distance.

Why I let you go…

And then it was gone. Every drop of the ocean of blood vanished, leaving him stranded in an urban mockery against a curtain of blackness. All around him the skyline held no promise of any concept of "beyond"—no stars nor moon nor hope—and he found himself staring at a vacant street that stretched infinitely both ahead and behind him. Only a short distance away, he spotted his only possible solace:
Serena!
Axle's eyes widened and he began to sprint down the road towards her, ignoring the tremors that once again threatened to rip the world apart.
None of that meant a damn thing to him. Nothing else mattered.
Throwing himself into a mad dash towards her, he rolled and vaulted and dove and duck under everything that the tremors dropped in his path.
A sedan—its wailing alarm fading in and out as it rolled towards him—was easily cleared as he kicked off from a runaway hotdog stand and barrel vaulted over the runaway car's hood.
Landing in a tucking roll, he caught sight of a portion of a building that threatened to block his path. Refusing to slow down, he pushed that much harder, the collapsing rooftop landing around him—boxing him within its weakened walls and threatening to dump its collapsing roof on top of him—and offering only a cracked window ahead of him to illuminate the space. Hurdling towards the single pane of glass, he threw himself into a screwdriver dive that freed him from the collapsing structure and sent him sailing into a new set of obstacles.
A sailing double kong over a picnic table.
Monkey vault between a set of concrete barricades.
The city came alive in an attempt to stop him from reaching Serena, who seemed to never be closer but never too far…
The ground ripped free and began to disappear beneath him, leaving Serena—his prize—growing ever distant at the bottom. Crying out her name, he flung himself over the edge in what he was sure was a suicidal air bomb and…
He landed, rolling with the momentum and pulling himself to his feet right in front of Serena.

The bed stretched across the meridian of the street; the wind-licked sheets gripped tightly in her hands as her naked body writhed and heaved in orgasmic pleasure just in front of him. She was so close...

He reached out, eager to escape the chaos of this world and sink into the bliss he saw in her.

"All the things you've done," Axle whispered to her as his hand wavered in the ether between him and her, "have made me fall in love with you."

Serena's silent orgasm rolled on before him, her sweat-glistening breasts heaving as she spread her sex before him; further inviting the invisible source of her pleasure.

And then his hand found the barrier.

An unseen wall that kept Serena just outside of his reach.

"I'll never know why I let you go, my love."

Looking up towards the source of the familiar voice, Axle spotted a man—his pitch-black hair interrupted by a single silver bang that hung between his silver and blue eyes—perched atop the barrier; squatting atop the massive, transparent cube that kept him from the only thing that mattered to him anymore.

"Who are you?"

"Who are you?"

"ANSWER ME!"

"ANSWER ME!"

"You..."

"You..."

"Can't..."

"Can't..."

"Have..."

"Have..."

"Her!"

"Her!"

The two roared at one another, their voices mirroring one another as though the thoughts emanated from a single source.

"I'm tired of trying..." Axle groaned, leaning his head against the barricade, "Serena, I would do anything to be lying with you..."

"I'm sick of waiting!" The man growled.

Then Serena was gone.

And, before Axle, only the man.

"You don't belong here," he growled, stepping towards him. "You don't belong with her!"

"WHAT WOULD YOU KNOW ABOUT IT?" Axle roared.

"More than you know," the man threw the first punch; a solid right hook that took Axle across the jaw and threw him to the road.

But no pain...

Somewhere behind him, Axle was somehow aware of one of the many buildings collapsing under its own weight.

"I've been forced to watch this scene, and all that's happened has led me—led us—to this bittersweet abyss. Now you need to go—you need to do what will set things right—or I will rip you out and do it myself."

In the distance, Serena's cries of ecstasy rose over the horizon, chanting a name that Axle couldn't bring himself to hear.

The man nodded, "Serena, close your eyes. I'll be your lover tonight." He sighed and looked up at Axle, "This is the lullaby to sing the tortured to sleep..." he charged towards him, "And you MUST sleep!"

Fists flew.

Feet struck.

Flesh and bone slammed with apocalyptic force.

And all around them the buildings crumbled and collapsed.

I have broken free! You hear me? I'm free! FREE!
You can't deny me; can't defy the truth!
I have been reborn!

"WHO ARE YOU??" Axle roared, throwing his elbow back in an attempt to catch his attacker in the skull, only to have him duck beneath the blow and deliver an uppercut to his gut.

And then Serena's voice called out, and the name rang like church bells across the eternity of their battlefield.

"ZANE!!!"

The man nodded, closing in on Axle as the buildings collapsed all around them, "Yes, my darling. I've been reborn. Tonight... we say goodbye!"

CHAPTER FOURTEEN
START OF SOMETHING GOOD

SERENA SIGHED AS SHE SAT IN her study, pretending—even to herself—to look over the accounts for the clan. Despite the responsibilities at hand, her mind was determined to keep her thoughts on only one thing.

Axle.

She growled after her mind replayed the scene of the kiss inside her head once again and she shook her head, pushing the paperwork aside. Sighing, she rested her head in her hands.

"Why did he kiss me...?" She whispered to herself.

Zane was still out there—somewhere—and though there was something in Axle that kept her second-glancing him, there was never a moment when her heart didn't know *exactly* where her loyalties lay.

Zane...

The one who had saved her; the one who had protected her.

The one who had loved her in ways that she'd never thought possible.

So what was it about Axle that kept the two names bobbing side-by-side?

What was she trying to tell herself?

A knock on the door jolted her from her thoughts and she quickly moved to answer it.

"Yes?" She blinked a few times as Zane's face greeted her, and forced herself several times to remind herself that it was Raith standing at the door.

"You got some time? I need to talk to you," he frowned.

"Uh, sure. I suppose that's not a problem. Do you want to come in?" She moved out of the way to let him through. After a moment of him not moving, she sighed and nodded, "Alright then! A walk it is!"

The walk was a quiet one through the city and Serena was beginning to worry that Raith wouldn't say a word to her at all.

She wanted to see Axle again and clear things up...

Turning to look at Raith, she found herself swept into memories of Zane.

"It must be hard, eh?" Raith finally said.

"Excuse me?" Serena found herself yanked back in the present. Back in the cold streets of the city. Back in the world where she didn't have Zane.

"To look at me, I mean. Having me squattin' in your man's body must be tough for ya," he frowned. "I just sort of feel like I should offer my sympathies. If it had been up to me it wouldn't have happened like this."

Serena looked over and nodded slowly, before offering a small smile. "Even so, it must've been hard for you as well. To watch through your friend's eyes. Especially Zane's... we all know he hasn't had the best of years."

"He's definitely a lot darker and more grim than he was before..." Raith sighed.

"Was he very different then? Before whatever happened to create *Maledictus*, I mean." Serena asked.

"Completely different! Granted, he was a still a fan of the ladies, but he was a gentleman and charmer back then. He was…" Raith sighed, "He was the sort of guy you wanted to have around no matter what, whether it was at the greatest of parties or the most vicious of battlefields. He had looks, charm and a positive attitude towards life." Raith sighed, "But after the Taroe… Well, it was all too much for him."

"I understand… and *Maledictus* certainly didn't help with his outlook on life," Serena shook her head, biting her lip and shivering, "We were surprised that… that *beast* had actually taken a liking to me."

"That *beast* doesn't know the difference between friend or foe, I'm afraid. What it felt—well, what it *feels*—for you can't really be defined by anybody. But what you showed it that when you first met Zane…" He shrugged.

Serena blushed and looked over, "So… you saw all of that then? That night and all the times that…"

Raith shrugged, "I don't want to make this awkward, but I don't want to lie to you either. There was a reason that *Maledictus* always talked about himself as 'us' and 'we'," he looked over and pointed to himself, "The curse needed all of us—Zane, me, *and* it—to become that thing; it was my therion heart that fueled the change each time. It's why, without him in here with us, *Maledictus* can't come out and I can't transform. This body is just a vampire body now." He pointed to his right eye, "And this has changed back to my normal eye color?"

Serena stared, "*Your* normal…"

Raith nodded, "Yup. The taroe were nothing if not thorough, I'm afraid. Part of the *Maledictus* curse was to choose a subject—Zane—and embody him with the means to 'carry' any accomplices with them. Along with my heart, they gave him my eye so I'd always be forced to watch the *Maledictus* while he committed his acts; we were condemned to watch side-by-side as the monster we created did what it was created to do." Raith sighed, "Now that a crucial part of the equation is gone, my eye is no longer empowered by the therion drive that fueled it, so it shines with the color of my human form."

Serena smiled, "I think it's pretty. You must have been really handsome."

"Nothin' compared to your boyfriend, sweetheart, but Nicc'oule seemed happy with the way I looked."

Serena nodded, still having to remind herself that their Nikki hadn't always gone by that name. "Well, I see the way she looks at you... well, not *you*, but you know what I mean. Anyway, I don't think it has much to do with looks with her."

Raith smiled, "But would it be any different for you if your Zane was in any other body?"

Serena paused on that a moment. "Any other body...?"

The sharp sound of a nearby trashcan smashing against the ground jolted both of them to their surroundings and they started towards an alleyway. Reaching the source of the commotion, they found nothing more than a vacant alley, a bunch of scattered trash...

And a partially skewed manhole cover.

"Oh come on..." Serena rolled her eyes. "They don't *really* expect me to go down there, do they?"

Raith frowned, "They?"

Serena nodded, "Whatever deities I've angered enough to be doing this..."

"Well," Raith yanked the giant metal slab away from the entrance into the sewer and started down into the depths, "just imagine the karma you're earning."

"Oh now *that* is just fucking wrong!" Serena's eyes widened as she took in the lizard-like appearance of the ykali stooping a short distance ahead of them.

The three reptilian creatures were mostly covered in baggy street clothes, but—for the sake of enjoying their meal—they'd drawn back the hoods and scarves that hid their scaly, hairless, protruding snouts and jagged teeth. Hearing the two drop down to the muck-soaked ground, the three had turned away from the body they'd been feasting on and had begun an appalling hymn of enraged hisses and dry, airy growls.

"Serena! I got the one on the right! Take the left and we'll get the middle together!"

Serena watched as Raith rushed towards the first ykali and she quickly turned her own target. Not wanting to touch the repulsive creature, she threw out her aura and shaped it into a bow that she "held" in her right hand. Though it was an unconventional method with others, the self-trained archery enthusiast had found a greater degree of control and focus in wielding her aura as a tangible, polymorphous weapon rather than a shapeless extension of herself. Drawing back her "arrow", she waited for the ykali to make its move and started a slow approach towards it. Snapping its jaws, the giant lizard lunged at her and she loosed the bright purple beam, letting it pierce through her attacker and hold it. With her aura still gripping the creature, she swung it around, using the "arm" of her auric limb to trip the third ykali in the center and bringing it towards Raith's opponent.

"GET DOWN!" Serena warned.

Not waiting to question her reasons, Raith ducked down and allowed the thrashing ykali impaled on the end of Serena's aura to crash into the first. As the two collided, the pair went into a panic-fueled berserker rage and began to slash and bite at the other.

By the time Serena expanded the auric hold within the ykali she'd "shot"—causing it to explode into leathery, scale-covered chunks—the damage to the first had rendered it as good as dead.

"Hells-fucking-yea, you walking purse-assed motherfuckers!" Serena cheered.

Raith turned to face her, "Did you just say 'purse-asse—LOOK OUT!"

The third ykali let out a loud ear-piercing shriek, and Serena threw her aura out in a blind hail Mary that only seemed to piss it off. Taking the hit to its chest, the creature rolled around the attack and began to run faster towards her as it threw out its greenish-brown fist into Serena's stomach. Serena cried out as she lurched forward from the punch before quickly recovering and swung her right foot out in a high kick that landed in the ykali's already injured chest.

"You gross fuck!" Serena glared as she threw out her right fist and directed her auric energies into the punch as she swung into the ykali's face over and over again before finally throwing an auric-empowered kick into its side.

The ykali shrieked and flew back, crashing into the brick wall of the far side of the tunnel—the sound of several of its bones breaking echoing—and fell into a large pool of filth.

Hearing a grunt, Serena looked over as the first ykali that she'd counted out of the fight earlier had continued its injury-induced rampage on Raith. Holding the snapping jaws back with his left forearm—which he'd lodged under the creature's chin and against the base of its throat—he repeatedly drove his right fist into the side of the monster's head. Casting out her aura, Serena threw the battered ykali from Raith and watched as he kicked to his feet and drove his fist through the ykali's chest. Letting out a startled gasp, the creature fell back—falling free of Raith's hand—and let them both see the still-beating heart that he'd earned in the process. Serena looked over and sneered for a moment at the sight of the dying organ.

"That's disgusting!"

"You want it?" Raith smirked, "It looks kind of cool!"

"Why do I get the idea that if you could," Serena wretched, "you'd jar that thing up and keep it?"

"I don't think Nicc'oule would appreciate that!" Raith laughed.

"I don't think anybody would!" Serena laughed and watched as he threw the heart on the ground and frowned at the body they'd been huddled around when they'd first arrived.

Unsurprisingly, the remains belonged to more of Axle's gang members.

"Where are these things coming from?" Raith frowned as he eyed the bodies too.

"I have a feeling this isn't an accident; any of it," Serena picked up her phone and called for a clean-up crew. When she was done, she turned to Raith, "Let's get back to the clan. I've got some questions that need answering."

When they finally got back, Zoey was waiting with Isaac and Nikki; their faces all holding what Serena already had been feeling: suspicion.

"None of this has been an accident," Serena explained. "These ykalis have been being used as some sort of weaponized distraction. There's somebody who is tracking down all of Axle's old friends and executing them, and these ykali 'attacks' have been a convenient cover story that puts the blame on them while simultaneously destroying any evidence that the *real* culprit might be leaving behind. Like a goddam serial killer feeding the corpses of their victims to the pigs. And there's only *two* things that have changed in our jurisdiction since this all began: the victim—Axle—and who I'm beginning to suspect has been behind this mess the entire time," Serena clenched her fists and looked up after a moment, "That new clan!"

"Serena, not again..." Zoey frowned.

"Zoey, I can promise you... I *will* find out what I need to know from that clan! Those fuckers haven't even allowed me to *see* their leader—hell, we *still* don't know who's running that show!—or even get inside enough to find out anything more!"

"Do you truly think they are responsible?" Isaac frowned.

"I do," Serena nodded, "And I wouldn't just push on this instinct if I didn't believe they had something to do with this!" Serena frowned, "Zoey... please, you've got to believe me."

"Alright, Serena," Zoey sighed and nodded, "Just don't get yourself into any trouble if they refuse to see you again."

"I make no promises." Serena smirked.

"I wasn't expecting you to," Zoey laughed. "If you had I would've known you were lying."

"Has Axle been around at all?" Serena frowned.

"No. I haven't seen him since last night," Zoey frowned.

Serena bit her lip and nodded slowly, "I think I need to go talk to him."

"You're back..." Axle stepped over as Serena let herself in.

"Y-yea, how'd you know I was gone," Serena asked, realizing he had been waiting for her.

"Could we... maybe spend some time together?" Axle frowned; ignoring Serena's question and looking down.

Serena noticed the confusion in his eyes and slowly nodded, "Sure. But is something wrong?"

"I..." He looked away, "I'm not sure."

As she watched him, he stepped over towards her and took her hand in his as if testing something. Still watching Axles experiment, Serena watched him study the sight of their clasped with an eye of familiarity.

"Come on, let's go," Serena smiled, keeping their hands laced and guiding him out of his room, "Let's go for another walk."

Though the idea of being alone with Axle with how he was acting made Serena nervous, she knew that, in the event that there was some volatile moment growing within him, it would be better to have him outside and *not* in an underground confinement where he could hurt himself or somebody else.

The moon was full, and though a part of Serena still liked to imagine that nights like this motivated the therions across the world to lose all control and explode into their bestial forms, the truth that, while *everybody* seemed to get a little crazy, it didn't play out like an old horror movies. Despite this, she wasn't entirely convinced that Axle wouldn't be an ironic catastrophe in the making.

As they navigated the moon-lit forest, Serena struggled to feel at peace for once. Looking over at her companion, however, made that effort an unlikely dream. Though the violent outburst she'd been working against didn't seem to be making an appearance, there was a definite war going on within him. Serena frowned; she wanted to make him feel better but had no idea what to do to help his situation.

"Is something wrong?"

"No, just...in thought." He smiled, "had another bad dream."

"Oh?" She tilted her head, "Can you tell me about it?"

"It's not important..." Axle frowned as the two continued to walk deeper into the woods.

His eyes continued to drift over her and she felt a shiver as she noted the possessive gaze he was giving her.

"Axle, why do you keep looking at me like tha—"

Serena's words were caught in her throat as she was pulled against him, pressing her to his chest.

"Serena... I want you."

"Axle? What are you saying?" She looked up, stunned by his sudden desire and force. "Stop this! This isn't you!"

"ISN'T ME? THEN WHAT *IS* ME? WHO AM I IF I'M

NOT WHO I AM?"

Serena narrowed his eyes, "Axle, don't make me punch you in the nose ag—MPH!"

His lips crashed down on hers and she felt...

Nothing.

The thrill and pleasure that his lips had held before were now nothing more than desperate jackhammers.

It was wrong.

And, most importantly, it wasn't Zane.

Zane was still out there!

She knew it now more than ever!

Extending her fangs, she bit down on his lip; releasing only when he yelped and tore his lips away from hers and cupped a hand over the two puncture wounds. His eyes widened as he saw the blood and he looked up at Serena, his eyes filled with torment and his stare oozing panic and confusion.

"Axle... you need to—"

"Zane..." He whimpered.

Serena's eyes widened, "What?"

"He... he came to me in my dream last night. He attacked me; said that I wasn't meant to be here and I had to make things right..." He looked up and wiped his already-healing lip again, "Who is he? What does he mean?"

Serena's lip quivered, "Zane... H-how can that..."

"I've lost to him... haven't I?" Axle looked up at her.

"Axle... there was *never* a competition. I've been looking for Zane ever since an accident took him away from me, and when I find him *he'll* be who I'm with," she stepped towards him, placing her hand on his shoulder.

"Then who am I?" Axle whimpered, shaking his head. "It... it felt so right being with you, like *that's* where I was meant to be..." He growled and his eyes flared with rage and his voice came out in a low growl, "WHO THE FUCK AM I?" He roared as he turned away from Serena and slammed his fist into a tree.

A thunderous crack echoed through the forest, scaring various pods of animals that scattered away from the source.

"Who am I...?" Axle whimpered, dropping to his knees as the tree collapsed onto the forest floor.

"Axle..." Serena frowned and stepped forward to try and calm him.

"Stay back," he groaned, "It feels too good to have you near me..."

She watched as his body began to shake and he clasped onto his head as he let out a loud scream. Suddenly, he fell to his knees still clutching his head in agony. Serena finally disregarded his order and stepped over, placing her hands on his shoulder.

"We need to get you some help," she frowned as another pained shudder wracked through his body. Serena helped to lift him and carried him back to the office, where Zoey and Isaac sat together going over some notes.

"Zoey!" Serena cried out, "I need your help!"

Finally, unable to hold him up any longer, Serena started to lose her grip and Axle started to fall forward. Isaac rose from his seat then, swooping in and catching Axle by the shoulders and the two frowned at Serena.

"What happened?" Isaac asked.

"I don't know," Serena whimpered. "He's been holding his head this entire time; complaining of headaches and telling me he doesn't know who he is!" Serena frowned and looked at Zoey, "Zoe! He's dreaming of Zane! How is that even possible?"

Raith and Nikki—clearly having heard the commotion—rushed into the room. As they approached the group, Raith cried out and clutched at his head, starting to cackle as tears of agony rolled down his face. Turning to try to offer some comfort to the suddenly hysterical Raith, Nikki's magical taroe tattoos sparked to life and began to glow brightly as she tried to work her magic to ease the situation.

Axle looked up through hazy eyes and smiled weakly at Isaac, "H-hey, Babe Ruth... you hit any home runs with that killer wood of yours recently..." stammering on the last syllable, Axle passed out.

"What the hell is going on?" Nikki's eyes widened.

"M-Maled—" Raith let out a loud, inhuman growl, "*Maledictus*! He's awake! He's awake and—AAHH! H-hee..." Raith smirked, his eyes drifting up in his head, "We want *him*!" He pointed a finger towards Axle, and as everyone watched in shock, the limb began to jerk and crack as the fingers began to break and shift—the finger slowly beginning to lengthen in Axle's direction.

"What the fuck?" Serena cried, "*Maledictus* has been inactive since Zane's been gone!"

"He's back!" Raith's voice came out in a rattling hiss, "He's back! He's back!" his eyes darted towards Serena, the right eye's iris beginning to shift to silver, "BA-A-A-A-*AAAACK!*" Raith howled and clutched his eye, a trail of blood beginning to seep from his right eye!

"G-get him out of here! Get me away from him! K-k-keep us apar—AAHH! FUCK YOU! FUCK YOU ALL! GIVE HIM TO US!! GIVE HIM TO US NOW OR WE'LL RAPE EACH AND EVERY ONE OF YOUR CORP—"

"SHUT UP, ASSHOLE!" Serena brought her two fists down on Raith's skull, knocking him out. Panting, she shook her head, "Haven't missed *his* ass one goddam bit!"

Zoey slid over to Axle and frowned as she placed a hand on his shoulder. "He's not Axle anymore," she explained, looking up at Serena. There's two conflicting personalities struggling for dominance, but neither is sure who they are or where they become the other.

Serena's eyes widened.

The dreams.

The obsessive behavior.

The rage…

She froze as she stared down at Axle, suddenly knowing that Zane had found his way home.

CHAPTER FIFTEEN
CLOSING IN

"SERENA?" AXLE'S EYES FLUTTERED open as Serena steered his convertible around a bus and merged back into the lane.

"Hey, sleepy-head," Serena offered a weak smile as she took the exit towards Sierra's orphanage. "Anybody ever tell you that you snore like a fucking bear? What is it with you therions and—"

"Where are we going?" Axle sat up in the seat and looked around.

Serena forced a scoff, fighting the urge to break out into tears, "I'd imagine *that* would be obvious!" She motioned ahead of them, where the dilapidated building's roof could be seen in the distance, "We're going to go visit our friends. It's been a while since you've seen the kids…" she glanced over, "And Sierra."

Axle's eyes lit up at the name; his shoulders and neck returning to the bouncy playfulness that she recognized as Axle's own.

"You like her, don't you?" Serena asked. "If I had to guess, I'd imagine you two went way back, am I right?"

Axle looked over and, blushing like a little boy, nodded. "We were in the orphanage together growing up. She wound up doing a lot of work for the younger kids, even helping the kitchen staff plan out the meals and doing whatever she could to raise funds so they had toys. The others used to pick on her—some even tried to beat her up a few times—and I started watching out for her," he looked over. "She called me her 'bodyguard', and I told her I'd always protect her." He nodded to himself, "I promised her every night that I'd never let anything bad happen to her."

"I'm surprised you didn't marry the girl," Serena played the role she knew he needed; the role of the bitch. If she let on that something was wrong—let it show how much she was torn up on the inside—then she'd risk losing him to another slip into his own mind.

And she wasn't sure if she'd ever get him back from that.

Whatever was left of Axle—the one, *true* Axle—was hanging on by less than a thread. If there was any hope of saving both him *and* Zane, then she had to play along and keep Axle from slipping away.

Axle blushed and nodded looking out at the passing scenery, "Can I tell you a secret?"

Serena nodded, "I guess. Unless you're coming out of the closet; too many of my gay friends come out to me 'cuz they think I'm a guy?"

Axle looked over, laughing, "They think *you're* a guy?"

"Well, not a guy in the 'traditional' sense," Serena let go of the wheel long enough to provide air quotes, "but they think that I have a dick and they hope that I'll serve as some sort of emotional bridge. So, naturally, I let them fuck me, and, I'll be honest, Axle, I'm not sure my heart can take another one of *those* kinds of relationships."

Axle stared at her. "Please tell me you're joking."

"Of course I'm joking!" Serena laughed before offering a slight shrug, "Nah, I fuck them!"

"What?" Axle started to laugh.

"Well, naturally. I mean, they just *came out!* They don't want to use a chick-with-a-dick like they'd use any other woman. They want a chick who can give it to 'em nice and hard while still providing a gorgeous feminine physique to look upon while they're getting reamed."

"You're disgusting." Axle announced, "You're disgusting, I'm in the car with a disgusting woman, and I want to be with my pure-hearted orphan friends and the innocent, beautiful woman of my dreams and completely forget this conversation ever took place."

"Oh stop pretending that you're all 'white knight' and shit! You and I *both* know that you'd love nothing better than to have me looming over you with a can of WD-40 and a spork."

Axle groaned, "What's the spork for?"

"If you have to ask," Serena looked over, "you don't wanna know."

They both laughed.

Though for outward appearances she was taking Axle to the orphanage for a long-overdue visit to both the kids he'd worked so hard to protect as well as his childhood sweetheart—something that Serena *also* hoped would motivate the part of Axle that was convinced he loved her, due to Zane's own feelings melding with his lingering personality, to remember who *truly* held his heart—it was, in fact, an act of precaution and closure. The goal, when everything was said and done, was to get Zane's aura moved back to his own body and to try and nurse what remained of Axle back to full strength. However, the threat of losing Axle in the process was too great a threat, and though Zoey had been insistent on acting immediately, Serena felt that it was only right that Sierra and the kids get to see Axle—the *real* Axle—before they risked losing him forever.

It was only right to offer them that closure.

However, there was a far greater worry lingering in Serena's mind.

Whoever had been tracking down and killing Axle's gang had been well informed. Well informed... and thorough. And while driving into a possible slaughterhouse with Axle was just about the worst set of circumstances Serena could imagine, the benefit that could be earned by the happy reunion *far* outweighed the threat of Axle's mind slipping away forever.

From what Zoey had told Serena, hitting a pothole the wrong way might be enough for that to happen.

"Driving a little slower than normal, huh princess?" Axle

teased, looking over.

Serena frowned and shrugged, "Well, you know, with gas prices what they are and all, how can you *not* do all you can to conserve our resources, right?"

Axle stared at her. "You're joking, right?"

"The environment's not a joking matter, jackass!" Serena stuck out her tongue.

"No. No it isn't," Axle nodded, "But you giving a shit about the environment *is* a matter that would only come up in jokes? So why are you *really* driving like an old lady all of a sudden?"

Serena sighed, "I've just got a lot on my mind with work and all."

"Anything you wanna talk about?" Axle looked over, the sincerity in his eyes nearly pushing Serena over the edge.

"Nah, nothing *that* important. Just trying to do right for you and Sierra and the kids while keeping the fact that I'm harboring a wanted criminal in my clan's walls secret from the bulk of my clan mates *and* the very, extremely nosy Council."

Axle chuckled, "Makes sense," he smiled, "Do you really think you'll be able to help Sierra and the kids?"

Serena nodded, "That's certainly the point of most of this. Which reminds me," she nodded towards the glove box in front of him, "Can you grab me something out of there? It's this little black box"—she chuckled—"my, *that* sounds cryptic when you're in a car with me, doesn't it?"

Axle laughed, "Like a black box would *survive* a crash with you driving."

The both cackled as Axle reached into the glove box and pulled out the small, black, velvet box.

"What is this?"

Serena smirked, "Open it."

Doing so, Axle's eyes widened as he took in the wedding ring that Serena had picked up a short time earlier while he'd been passed out in his auric-induced sleep. After convincing Zoey to help her probe Axle's unconscious mind for the details to his and Sierra's history, his dreams—dreams of getting out of trouble with The Council and finally establishing himself in a role that would allow him to finally propose to the girl he'd grown up with—and to figure out what *one* gesture would genuinely push for the best to come of things.

Though Serena and Zoey agreed that using their mind-reading abilities to create the *perfect* romantic scenario between the two was pretty cheap, Serena figured that shelling out a few extra thousand dollars on the ring would balance things out.

"Wh-what is this?" Axle stammered.

Serena rolled her eyes, "Well clearly you're not a golfer."

"Huh?"

Serena shook her head, mumbling about "uncultured therions" before she nodded towards the ring. "I got a deal for ya, stud."

Axle bit his lip, "What would that be?"

"I'm sort of a sucker for happy endings and all, but I'm also sort of a manipulative bitch. So, what I'm going to do is move you, your lady friend, *and* all the kids into the Vail Clan's headquarters as official, registered members. I'll push all the paperwork to have your history forgiven—explaining that you were trying to care for these unfortunate children and that I'm personally taking responsibility for your rehabilitation and helping to repay whatever losses for whatever shit you and your boys made off with in your all your fun-havings."

As Serena's explanation went on, Axle's eyes grew wider and wider until she was certain they would fall out of his skull. "S-so what's the catch? I... I mean, you *did* say this was all part of some deal, right?"

Serena nodded, "Right you are, sport. So, as you can see, I'm busting a *fuck-ton* of awesome, life-changing shit on your lap, right?"

"R-right..." Axle answered, obviously nervous about what was coming.

"So what I want from you—and what you'll fucking *give* to me if you expect *any* of this fairy tale bullshit to come true—is that when we get there," Serena looked over and nodded at the ring, "you drop on your knee in *true* old-skool fashion and deliver the single most heart-warming, birds singing, roses blossoming, church bells tolling, panty dropping, condom-popping speech that you can come up with and ask Sierra to marry you. If I'm going to offer a life-changing experience, you need to take a life-changing step in return." Serena took a deep breath and offered a sidelong glance, "So we got a—boy, tell me are you not *crying* all over that ring!"

"Axle! S'rena!" Fang cried out happily and charged the door as the two of them stepped inside.

Catching the little vampire in mid-leap, Axle laughed and rustled the boy's hair, "There's my little buddy," he rustled the boy's hair. "Have you been behaving while I was gone?"

Fang smiled and nodded, "Of course!"

Axle raised an eyebrow. "Oh? Have you bitten anybody?"

Fang smiled and nodded, "Of course!"

Both Serena and Axle couldn't hold back their bouts of laughter as they walked deeper into the building.

"So where is everybody?" Serena asked.

Fang giggled.

"What is it?" Axle looked down at the boy.

Another giggle.

"Fang? Is somebody keeping secrets?" Axle tickled the boy, earning a fit of giggles and writhes. "Come on! Fess up, kid! What secrets are you hiding?"

"Sierra and the others are in the other room waiting to surprise you!" Fang announced.

A short way's away, the sound of all the kids groaning at their blown cover grew and they stormed out to chide their friend about ruining surprises.

"In Fang's defense," Serena offered, pointing a thumb back at Axle, "this one wouldn't let him keep the secret! Fang tried; I saw!" She nodded, "I say if *anybody* deserves to be punished, then I'd say it's *him*." She smirked and knelt down, "And I've *always* believed that the best punishment is to return the crime that earned it, which is why I propose…" Serena stood and pointed at Axle, "…DEATH BY TICKLES!"

There was a sudden hush inside of the room, and Serena watched as the combined auras of all the children swelled into a technicolor singularity that shifted towards Axle like a tidal wave before each and every child charged forward, issuing their playful battle cries as they attacked.

Despite all the skill that Serena had seen Axle exhibit in the time she'd known him—despite all his wit and cunning and speed and claims to be elusive and uncatchable—and despite the fact that his opponents were only small children, Axle was unable to remain standing under the onslaught.

A moment later, Sierra stepped out, blushing at the sight of the mountain of kids and joined Serena at her side.

"It was nice of you to arrange this for the kids," she blushed, looking down and stammering as though she were addressing royalty. "It really means a lot to them, and... to me."

Serena smirked and bumped Sierra with her hip, "Come on, girl! You're *way* too tense! You're allowed to show excitement once in a while," she nodded towards the kids. "Just look at them, they aren't all quiet and reserved! They're loving on life!" Serena smiled, "And they're loving on life *because* of what you've done for them. You've done more for those kids than most people—no matter how long they live—can do for *anybody* in their lifetime! Have some pride in your work and in yourself." Serena leaned against the wall, "besides, Axle's pretty much a giant, parkour-practicing five year old, so you'd better be ready to babysit that boy for, like, ever," she smirked.

Sierra blushed and shrugged, "Aw, what the hell!"

With that she pulled her hair out of the tight bun over her head—letting her gorgeous black mane cascade over her shoulders—and joined the kids in the dog pile to tickle Axle, the first sincere laughter rolls of laughter beginning to issue from her lungs.

It was nearly twenty minutes before Serena had even *tried* to dig Axle out from under the tickle-happy kids. By the time she and Sierra had successfully exhumed the beet-red and panting therion, he'd completely drenched his face in tears and his voice was raspy and hushed from laughing so hard.

At that time, Serena nodded to him and began to herd the kids into the other room, asking them to show her their toys so that Axle and Miss Sierra could have a moment alone. As the last of the orphans waddled into the other room, Serena leaned in to close the doors and offered a wink to the already nervous and panting Axle.

No sooner had the latch on the door sounded then their lips collided in a passionate frenzy that made up for every day they'd been apart with the sheer intensity of the moment. There was no question of morals or obligations or priorities; Serena—nothing short of a princess from a fairy tale—had appeared at their doorstep at their darkest hour and offered the orphans the lives they deserved.

Axle's record. Sierra's debt. All of their anxieties.

Gone.

And with that combined weight lifted from their shoulders by Serena Vailean, their kiss was free to rise to levels of passion and euphoria they'd have never thought possible.

It was only when their combined need for air finally became too urgent did they finally pull themselves from the other; both looking momentary lost with the sudden shift.

That was when Axle lowered himself to one knee.

Serena winced as the sharp cry and elongated wail carried over from the other room.

"Is that Miss Sierra?"

"Do you think she's hurt?"

"It sounds like she's yelling at Mister Axle…"

"Oh you've gotta be—" Serena caught herself for the sake of the kids and smiled, "It's alright, kids. I'm going to go check on them, okay?" Starting towards the door, Serena held back the wave of obscenities that bubbled within her.

He'd *botched* it?

She'd practically handed a successful proposal to the doofus on a silver platter and he *botched* it?

If he wasn't already dead from embarrassment, she was going to kill him.

Stepping through the door, Serena felt her fists already clenched at her sides and spotted the two of them locked in an embrace; Sierra sobbing—her aura rolling happily over her—and Axle holding her tight enough to make her excited cries come out hoarse and, from the other room, sound like wails of misery.

Serena smirked.
Maybe she'd let him live, after all.

"You have to leave so soon?" Sierra pouted.

Axle nodded, biting his lip, "There's something I have to help Serena with before we can get you and the kids moved over."

Though it was clear Sierra didn't understand, she offered a nod and absently began rubbing her left ring finger, where the wedding ring now rested happily.

Serena smiled reassuringly and gave Sierra a tight hug, "It won't be long. Just a few final renovations and such." She smirked, "You and the kids might want to start getting packed."

CHAPTER SIXTEEN
BREAK THE SPELL

"Z-ZANE?" SERENA WHISPERED, SEEING Axle's eyes open, "Is that you?"

"I'm... I'm back?" He looked around and frowned.

Serena's eyes widened—tears already streaming down her face—and she threw her arms around him, "Oh my god! It's really you!" She sobbed, burying his face in his shoulder and hooking her fingers into his back, "I missed you... I missed you so much, Zane... I'm sorry... I didn't mean to let her take you! I'm sorry... I just missed you so much!"

"Whoa, hey! It's okay, babes. I'm here now. It's alright," Zane put his arms around her and held her close, whispering in her ear. "It wasn't your fault. You did great." As he looked around the room, his eyes fell on Raith, who was standing nearby in his body, "What the fuck?"

Serena, tears still running down her face, glanced over her shoulder and, when she saw what he was confused about, let out a fractured giggle.

"It's me, buddy," Raith grinned, "And if you don't recognize this Aussie accent then you're just as thick-skulled as you've always been," he smirked, "Even *with* somebody else's skull."

"Raith?" Zane's eyes widened and he grinned. As Serena stepped aside for the reunion, Zane rushed in to give Raith a tight brotherly hug, "Oh man, I thought you were dead! I didn't mean to freak out there, I've just never seen you looking so good."

They laughed.

"No. Not dead, my friend. Just inside you!" Raith laughed.

"That sounds way dirtier than it should," Nikki laughed.

"Though, given the gathering, not entirely unexpected," Zoey chimed.

Isaac chuckled, "I wonder if he's still got any jokes in him now that he's in a therion's body, himself."

Serena bit her lip and stepped forward, "Zane... How *did* you end up in Axle's body?"

"I..." He frowned, "I've been in his body for quite some time..." He shook his head, his eyes showed his growing confusion.

"It's alright." Serena smiled, "you'll remember soon enough."

"That's why you felt drawn to him, Serena! You *sensed* Zane's aura in him after the shift was made!" Zoey smiled.

"Holy shit! You're right..." Serena's eyes widened. "When I caught Axle for the second time, he seemed different—the way he moved and the way he stood! And *that's* when I started to feel differently about him!" Serena turned to Zane, "Your aura must've gotten inside him somehow!"

"Speaking of which," Zoey smiled and stepped over, "Now that both your aura and body are in one place, I can put you back in your rightful body, Zane." She smiled over at Raith and nodded, "And I can transfer you into Axle's body."

"You can?" Serena's eyes widened.

"I delved in some magic," Zoey grinned, "and with Nikki at my side the energy swap will be a snap."

Nikki smiled and wrapped her arms around Raith, "did you hear that? You'll get to be a therion again!"

"And none too soon, either," Zane groaned, patting his crotch. "this things making me feel like a damn tripod!" He scoffed at Raith and Isaac, "I honestly don't know how your kind can even stand with these ridiculous things

"Well, then...let's begin!" Zane smirked.

Zoey smirked and nodded, "Yes! Let's!"

Zane frowned, "Wait..."

Everyone looked over.

"What about..." he touched a hand to his chest, "I mean, I'm glad I'm back—and I'm goddam *thrilled* to hear that you guys can make everything right—but what about Axle? What's going to happen to him?"

Serena bit her lip and turned away, a small whimper seeping past her lips as she fell against Zoey.

Sighing, Zoey wrapped her arms around her friend and looked up at Zane. "He didn't make it back," she explained. "Serena took him to see his fiancé and the orphans that he'd been caring for—she was hoping that there might be a chance to save both of you, but decided it would be safer to offer them some sense of closure in case something *did* go wrong—and, on the way back, he fell asleep. By the time Serena got back with him and brought him to us, his orange aura was gone; replaced by yours."

Zane frowned, "he... died?"

Zoey nodded, "Whatever happened to him—whatever put you inside him—did a lot of damage to his aura in the process. When your dormant aura found Serena, you began to wake up and, as your aura grew stronger, it began to consume and merge with Axle's. Eventually, you two were more a single mind than two, and as things went on it became that much more vague of where 'Axle' ended and 'Zane' began..."

Nikki nodded, "You'd nearly completely taken over to the point where even *Maledictus* could sense you in him." She motioned to Raith, "Soon as you two were close enough, that crazy bastard came out of hibernation and went into a frenzy to try and take you back so he could be whole again."

Zane sneered, "*Maledictus*? He's still alive in there?"

"He never stopped," Raith confessed, "but without your aura to fuel the process, the curse lay dormant."

"So why isn't he going crazy now? I mean, he's here, I'm here; shouldn't things be... you know, crazy?"

Serena sniffed and shook her head, glancing back, "I knocked him out when he started to go crazy."

Zane raised an eyebrow, "You knocked out *Maledictus* when he woke up?"

Raith laughed and nodded, "You bet your ass she did!" He rubbed his head, "And you'll have the lump to prove it soon enough!"

"No..." Zane shook his head.

Serena frowned, "What do you mean 'no'?"

Zane backed away from Raith, "I mean I'm not going back in there if that thing is still alive! I... I can't; I won't!"

Serena bit her lip, "But—"

Zane looked at her, "Baby, I'm... I'm sorry. You know I'd do anything—fucking *anything*—for you! But what's in that body... it... it's done things—made *me* do things—that can *never* be undone! You can't ask me to just climb into a cage with that sort of monster..." He sat down on the chair he'd woken up in and shivered, scratching at the phantom tattoos that had begun to burn on his shoulder.

Nikki narrowed her eyes at the gesture before looking at Raith's arms—studying the intricate tribal tattoos of her people that had bonded the *Maledictus* curse to him—and, finally, she looked back at Zane.

"If I can get you your body to you *without* the curse, would you go back to your body?"

Zane looked up at her, "What are you saying? There is no cure for the *Male*—"

"I'm not talking about a cure," Nikki smirked, "I'm talking about the chance to be rid of that monster once and for all, and the chance to *kill* it with your own two hands."

Serena blushed, "Nikki?"

Nikki nodded to her, "Get me a body, Goldi-fucks. And make sure it's ugly enough to hold what I'm going to be putting in it!"

Serena frowned, waiting by the door as Zoey and Nikki worked the ceremony.

"Serena?" Zoey's head popped out of the door and she smiled, seeing Serena's look of concern. "It's fine. Zane's out in the back, waiting for you."

Serena nodded, not wasting any time as she jumped into overdrive and rushed towards the forest to find Zane.

Spotting him—the *real* him; standing and waiting in his own body—leaning against a tree, she couldn't bring herself to drop out of overdrive or stop.

Instead, she allowed herself to crash into him at full force.

The momentum carried them both off their feet—a deafening roar echoing as a shockwave emanated from the site he'd been standing and tore several of the trees from the ground—and they slammed into the ground with enough force to skip and roll and dig up the earth like a bullet had been shot into the dirt. As their bodies crashed and slammed across the forest floor, they wrapped their arms around each other and kissed one another with an intensity that put their careening bodies to shame. When they'd finally skidded to a stop, Serena pulled back briefly.

"Are... are you hurt?" She asked.

Zane shook his head.

Serena beamed, "Good. That means I can be rough with you."

As he looked up at her, his mismatched gaze—the brown and blue she'd come to recognize over the past few months; a sign that the *Maledictus* curse was truly gone—glimmered with his familiar charm and he pulled her back to him.

CHAPTER SEVENTEEN
MOON DANCE

"I CAN'T BELIEVE HOW MUCH I missed you. It was, like, making me crazy-*retarded*!" Serena held Zane's arm tightly to her as they headed through the forest and she smiled, leaning against him.

"Wow! You're awfully affectionate, huh? Maybe I should disappear more often," he chuckled.

Serena hauled back and punched him in the arm as they stopped in a clearing in the forest that was filled with fireflies that lit the clearing showing the greens, blue and purples that had begun to glow off of the flowers and grass. "You *ever* do something like that to me again, and I'm gonna make *Maledictus* look like an appetizer to this world!"

"Holy shit," Zane nodded slowly, "Well then, for the sake of the world, I must be certain to never allow myself to be killed or injured on an auric level ever again."

Serena giggled, "You'd better fucking believe it." She smiled at him and kissed his arm where she'd punched him, taking in the sight of the tribal tattoos that were now *just* that: only tattoos. "What's it like now that he's gone?"

Zane followed her gaze to the taroe ink and studied the tattoos with a new eye, "Well, for starters I guess I can start appreciating these things a little more."

Serena smirked, "Oh? Then maybe we can talk about me getting one without you throwing a fit?"

Zane laughed and shrugged, "I suppose that's fair. Though I think I'm about two-hundred ahead of you?"

"Challenge accepted," Serena nodded.

"So did Zoey or Nikki say when he'll wake up?" Zane looked over.

Serena chuckled, "You're pretty eager to see *Maledictus* stand in his own body, huh?"

Zane frowned, "Only so I can cut him down once and for all," he scoffed, "I *still* can't believe you put him in an ykali's body."

"Really?" Serena rolled her eyes, "Ugly monster deserved an ugly monster body. Now you don't even have to see that thing as a person when it wakes up."

"Good thinking," Zane nodded, staring off into the distance, his blue aura shifting and rolling with a level of confidence that he'd never before been able to muster.

Seeing him like that just made the moment seem that much more perfect, "Kiss me, Zane."

Leaning down, he pressed his lips hard to hers, the emotion that had been hidden for so long—for too damn long—once again engulfed the two. The sound of rain began to patter around them and, as they were drenched in the heavy rain, they began to undress one another.

As Serena's aura whipped around in a passionate frenzy, the rain around them began to sizzle from the heat and steam wrapped around their bodies as more and more skin became accessible. Zane's shirt was the first to go as Serena ripped it open, exposing his toned and tattooed chest.

"I don't know how long I'll be able to last…" He confessed.

"It doesn't matter; it'll be long enough! Just take me!" Serena gasped in pleasure. "It's been *too damn long* for *both* of us!" She gasped as he pressed her against an oak tree, covered in the oak's leafy embrace, the steaming rain continued to pelt around them, shrouding their passion in a misty visage.

Zane's hands explored Serena's body, reacquainting himself with every contour of her form as more and more clothes fell to the forest floor.

"Oh fuck! Yes, I missed this so much, baby!" Serena cried out as his mouth found her left nipple and he let his fangs pierce her.

The sudden sting was quickly masked by a throbbing heat as his tongue went to work; his hands continuing to explore her hips and back.

As Zane pushed her further back against the tree, her legs wrapped tightly around his waist as his iron-hard member throbbed against her soaking-wet folds. With neither interested in prolonging their union any longer, each thrust against the other; embedding-slash-enveloping one another in one single moment of synchronicity. The ferocity and passion that had come to define their day carried over in their love-making as both gasped and moaned at the intensified efforts that the other offered as a tribute to their long overdue coital bliss.

Zane growled and locked his lustful gaze with hers, the glow in his mismatched eyes announcing his impending release and, seeing before her what she'd dreamed of for so long, Serena joined him and they shook with pleasure as the scalding wetness that surrounded them was mimicked from within.

Their heavy breaths continued as they held the other in their embrace, neither one having the energy, nor the desire, to break their grip.

"Never leave me again..." Serena repeated as she nuzzled her face into Zane's broad chest.

"I won't, but you gotta promise the same," Zane leaned down and kissed her head softly.

Serena nodded, "I promise... I'm not going anywhere."

As the rain began to die down, the two finally finished catching their breaths and, though reluctantly, parted so that they could retrieve their clothes.

"I *so* don't want to leave this moment," Serena confessed. "Everything beyond *this* is total fucking chaos."

"I know, babes," Zane frowned. "I feel the same..."

"There's a fat fucking 'but' looming overhead, isn't there?" Serena sighed.

"Yeah. There is: it's what we have to, Serena. You're stronger than ever and I'm back with the sort of vengeance that Hollywood makes movies about," he smirked, "together we'll be unstoppable. And we *both* know there's some major fuck-wads with an even more major ass-kicking coming their way."

Serena smirked, "Would you believe I *almost* forgot what a brilliant dirty talker you were?"

"Yea, well… you're not too shabby yourself."

As they headed back to the clan, the two held the other as close and Serena sighed, things were finally starting to look up.

"Serena! You're back!" Zoey cried as she rushed out with Isaac.

"What's up, Zoey?" Serena frowned.

Zane stepped forward, "Is *Maledictus* awake?"

Zoey bit her lip and shook her head, "Not yet, but we *were* able to track the ykalis' next move!"

"What? Where?" Serena glared.

"A run down building. We didn't understand why at first, but there's kids in there! It's filled with mythos children!"

Serena growled, "The orphanage! They must have traced Axle back to it…" She punched the nearby wall; not batting an eyelash when her fist erupted through the other side, "Those fuckers! They must have tailed me when I brought him there earlier! Isaac! You and Zoey take my bike! I don't care what you do to the bike—blow the damn engine to shit for all I care—but you get that speedometer to peak and you don't let it drop one single cunt hair or I'll fucking hack your balls off! Zoey, keep the cops off his ass and the assholes in the slow lane; you keep that aura moving double-time! Zane, you've got two minutes starting NOW to get yourself, Nikki and Raith suited up and waiting in the fastest car the garage is holding. If you don't have the keys, you hotwire that fucker. If the owner tries to stop you, kill them; I'll bury the body later. Any and all available warriors had better be prepped and briefed by the time I have my left boot buckled, otherwise they're inviting my root boot up their ass! Now let's go!"

CHAPTER EIGHTEEN
RISING DARKNESS

AS THE GROUP REACHED THE orphanage, they could already hear the screams of the children as the ykali attacked.

"How many are there, Zoey?" Serena frowned as she jumped out of the car and started towards the building.

"Six or seven at most. It looks like there was more, but they're ripping their own apart in there! They've gone into a berserker state. Be careful!"

"Good call, Zoe! You and Nikki take the high road! Isaac and Raith, join us when you're wearing something sharper! GO!"

Serena rushed to the entrance with Zane right behind her. Near the entrance, Serena spotted Sierra's body lying on the ground by the entrance and fought the urge to check for any signs of life; she could already see there were none. Biting her lip, she pushed past the body and threw out her aura.

"When you're in there, you focus on keeping those kids alive!"

"Got it," Zane nodded. "You got the door?"

"Not quite," Serena snarled.

Most of the front-facing wall burst inward as Serena drove her aura into the side of the building, as the sudden burst of debris threw the ykali frenzy off, she and Zane jumped into overdrive and rocketed into the building. Zane went to work snatching the kids that were time-frozen in their moments of panic and getting them safely outside. Matching his efforts halfway, Serena kept her focus on the chunks of debris that floated about overhead, using her aura to redirect the portions that posed a threat to those that she *didn't* want to see wearing the fragments in their skulls. As the orphans stopped being a risk, both of the vampires dropped out of overdrive.

On your six! Zoey's voice rang inside her head and Serena threw her foot back and caught one of the giant lizard mythos in the throat before Zane appeared behind it with a length of wiring and began to choke it.

Overhead, a bright blue auric bubble carried Zoey and Nikki to the second level at the top of the staircase—an auric tendril sweeping out and cutting one of the ykali's legs off before Nikki dropped down and embedded her twin sais into either side of the teetering monster's neck.

"Wolf pack incoming," Nikki announced, her taroe tattoos glowing brightly under her Kevlar vest.

Both Isaac and Raith barked out in unison—announcing their arrival—as they charged in and let loose a pair of howls that stopped *every* heartbeat in the building for a split second.

At that moment, the ykalis' lizard brains registered with *true* panic.

"S'RENA!"

Serena quickly honed on the familiar voice and she rushed forward, avoiding overdrive and scanning ahead of her to hone in on where the source was coming from.

"BELOW YOU!" Zoey called out.

Spotting a vent grate the fed into the boiler room, Serena took a page from Axle's parkour book and dropped into a slide that carried her through past the panel—her aura tearing the vent plate free from the wall before she crashed into it—and down the vent shaft. Spotting the ykali that was tracking Fang, she threw her aura out, wrapping the ykali in a tight purple bind, crushing its lungs from inside its chest as she ran past and scooped up the sobbing vampire boy and returned to the upper level.

"Fang, you need to get as many of the others that you can and get them outside, okay? There's bad things—real bad—but you gotta be brave for everyone and trust us to keep you all safe, okay? We'll stop them!"

Despite his terror, the little vampire nodded.

She smiled, "That'a boy! Go now! We'll find you soon!" Fang nodded and vanished into overdrive, leaving Serena to blink is awe. "Wow… who knew."

Turning back, Serena watched as Zane smashed his fist into the ykali's face, caving in half its skull.

"THERE'S MORE OF THEM COMING IN!" Nikki announced, her tattoos glowing and an overhead beam tearing free and falling on three ykali that were stalking after her. Though two were killed instantly, the third hissed and dragged the upper half of its body—the only half *not* crushed beneath the beam—and shrieked in surprise as Nikki brought her boot down on its neck.

"Looks like they're coming to us then!" Serena grinned.

Isaac and Raith appeared beside Serena and Zane then, standing at their full heights and roaring.

"Fuckin' A!" Zane smirked.

As a particularly daring ykali tried to drop down on Serena, Raith pulled the flailing monster out of the air and tore its arms out at the shoulders before taking it by the ankles and swinging it at breakneck speed into another who had a similar idea. Both hit the ground dead a moment later.

"Hey, Ink-doll! Zoey!" Serena beckoned.

Nikki smirked, "Talk to me, Goldi-fucks!"

"I'm here!" Zoey called back, casually using her unique, ballet-like martial arts to twirl and duck below the ongoing attacks of three Ykali.

Serena chuckled, "I think we might actually score some decent purses out of all this."

All three girls laughed.

Zoey giggled, "I think Isaac might need a new belt," she chimed in as she ducked backwards beneath a swiping claw and brought her foot up in a high kick that separated an ykali with its lower jaw. Returning to an upright position, her blue aura forked off; the first coiling around a lunging ykali and crushing it until the creature resembled a nearly empty toothpaste tube, while the second barreled into an ykali at her right and sending it hurtling into a hanging portion of the upstairs railing that had been severed when Nikki and brought down the beam. As the impaled carcass weighed the beam, it slowly bent downward, allowing the carcass to slide free and slam into the ground.

Barking his laughter at Zoey's offer, Isaac side-swiped a pair of ykali who tried to tackle him, only find themselves underfoot and under claw.

"Just leave enough for a wallet!" Zane rushed in, leaping over Isaac and coming down hard on another two; taking each one by the throats and beginning to crush their windpipes in his palms.

Serena smirked as her colleagues—her *friends*—converged and brought the fight to a close. As the last two made a mad dash for an exit, she "fired" a pair of auric arrows that pierced their backs and crushed their hearts in one pass.

She smirked over at Zoey, "Just like castrating a mouse from a hundred meters away, huh?"

"You've *definitely* earned a Snickers bar!" Zoey smiled.

"S'Renaaa!!" The loud cry startled Serena as she saw Fang rushing towards her.

"Fang!" Serena called back and turned to face the little vampire as she enveloped him in her arms. "It's alright now, Fang…where are the others?"

"They're hiding over there!" He pointed, "We all wanted to watch you fight!"

Serena frowned, "You should've been more careful! Besides, all this blood and guts is"—she paused for effect and then smirked—"pretty awesome, huh?"

Serena nodded and turned to Zoey and the others, biting her lip for a moment as she noticed Sierra's body once again and sighed. *Zoey, can you do something about that? The kids don't need to—*

It's already hidden from their sights, Zoey responded, *I saw in your mind that she was the one in charge and figured it would be better if they didn't see.*

You rock, Zoe. Think you can get a ride for all these kids lined up for me?

I already have.

Serena chuckled and shook her head, *You rock double-time!*

I know, Zoey giggled, *It's a curse, really.*

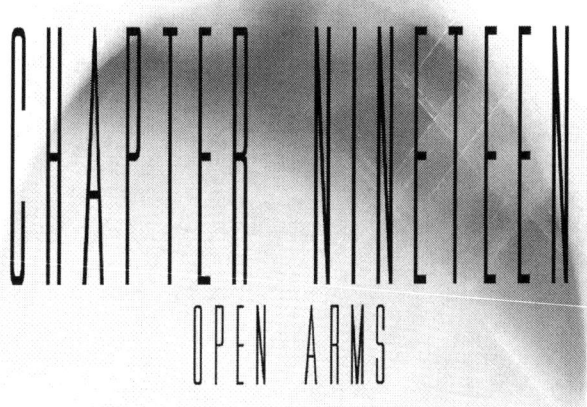

CHAPTER NINETEEN
OPEN ARMS

"RAITH," NIKKI WHISPERED AS SHE FELL into the new-yet-familiar embrace of Raith's new body, "Oh, how I missed this!"

Raith's arms pressed her to him as he traced his fingertips across her tattoos. She closed her eyes, basking in the contact and enjoying having a body for Raith. Finally back in a body that they could freely use.

No limitations.

No restrictions.

It was as it had once been.

Nikki moved her face upwards to look into the new, dark-green eyes that were now Raith's. Luckily, though there *were* some unmistakable differences, Axle's body was close in resemblance to Raith in the long run that Nikki found it incredibly easy to accept the new him.

It truly was a lucky match.

"Nicc'oule…" He sighed, placing his face into her hair, nuzzling her in the way he used to always do. "Ah! I've missed your scent. It's spicy and sweet all at once," he smiled. "Like cinnamon."

She giggled at that and leaned forward, "Bet you won't look at one of those cinnamon lattes the same way again, will you?" Smiling, she leaned into his embrace until she realized that, no matter how tightly he held her, it wouldn't satisfy what they were both after. "Do you remember our rock?" She cooed.

Raith smirked, "I do. Very much, actually." He chuckled.

"I think we should christen this new body." She looked up at him, "Just like you christened me on that rock all those years ago."

"Oh? Are you sure you're ready?" He smirked, his eyes gleaming in the darkness.

"Does this answer your question?" She pressed her chest upward—her cleavage pressing against her top—and the exposed tattoos already beginning to glow.

Raith needed no further incentive and pulled open her shirt with a sharp tug. Nikki gasped as her exposed chest met the open air, and she felt her nipples harden under Raith's intense gaze and the anticipation of what was about to come. Soon, Raith's hot breath replaced the slight chill on her hardened buds and Nikki pushed herself against his passionate kiss on her breasts. She gasped as his teeth grazed her sensitive buds and she shivered as he continued his onslaught on not only her nipples, but everything inch surrounding them.

She gasped out as his head moved up so he could get a better look into her eyes. "I'll never stop loving you, Raith."

"Nor I, you, Nicc'oule," he whispered. "This moment is making all the waiting worthwhile."

As their desire erupted into the room, their bodies collided into a fervent onslaught as they fought to relieve the built-up passion that resonated into their beings.

The two were *finally* together.

Finally one once again after so long.

Finally able to show the other how much their love still resounded in the other.

CHAPTER TWENTY
DARK AND STORMY

SERENA SMIRKED, "THAT'S IT! I'VE got the exact plan that can help us nail those bastards?"

"And which bastards might those be?" Zoey looked up.

"That new clan, of course!" Serena rolled her eyes.

Zoey stuck out her tongue, "Ah yes. Sorry; so much anarchy, so little time."

"New clan?" Zane frowned, "What do you mean 'new clan'? *We're* the clan here! What would they need to build another one for?"

"A new clan moved into town while you were 'indisposed'." Zoey sighed, "And Serena feels there's something not right about them."

"Fuckin' A, I do! Because it's the truth, Zoe! Let's look at the fucking facts: they pop up the goddam *moment* Axle and his gang shows up to help Sierra with her orphanage and, despite a limited criminal history, his fucking file gets pushed up as though it were some sort of priority. However, what the fuck have they done since then? Ever since putting forth a massive effort to establish themselves in less than *two days* they suddenly go quiet and do precisely *dick*; I mean, they have made made *zero* contact with us nor have we seen any sort of activity from them. Then, though they're doing *nothing* in the realm of patrolling to *prevent* such things, we see an unprecedented spike in not only illegal auric assignments to still-living subjects *and* an entire goddam nest of six-foot scaly, hissing cock-scabs that start ripping only a select group of not-so-bad 'bad guys' and a goddam *orphanage* to shreds. I've now visited the building on countless occasions, and I've yet to make it past the front desk because they insist that their leader who—unless you're keeping something from me, Zoe—we don't know the identity of? Aren't clan leaders, y'know, a relevant nugget of 'perhaps-I-should-fucking-know-that'-ness?" Serena sighed, "Not that I can do a goddam thing to prove it—or any of this, as far as you're concerned—but I'm pretty damn sure that they've got something to do with what happened to Zane, too!"

"To be fair, Zoey, she *does* have a point. The Council has trusted the Vail Clan for *decades*, but not one month after they suddenly decide to assign a second one and all this goes down? Not that I've ever been the political type, but shouldn't *more* law equal *less* crime?" Zane sighed, "Plus, Serena hasn't mentioned that all of this ALL happened exclusively when I was gone? For fuck's sake, how long has it been?"

"Four months..." Serena sighed, "And it's not like I was just flicking the bean while you were gone, either! I did get the clan's headquarters rebuilt and in great shape and!" She smirked, "I was able to get new members and keep the streets clean. UNTIL, that is, those fucking fuck-wads showed up and fucked it up!"

Zane shook his head, "That's not just fucking coincidence!"

Zoey sighed, "I'm noticing an exponential increase in the use of the word 'fuck' since your return, Zane."

"That's not just fucking coincidence either, Zoey," he smirked.

"Told you!" Serena smirked over at Zoey.

"So what do we do about it?" Zoey frowned.

"We go there in good, ol' fashioned Serena style!"

"That doesn't sound good," Zoey frowned.

Isaac stepped inside and smirked widely, "I think it'll be fun! I've been aching to get some fighting done!"

"Of course *you* would be, Isaac!" Zoey sighed. "Isn't there a more peaceful option?"

Zane frowned, "We haven't exactly had a peaceful few months, Zoey."

"We've tried peace, Zoey! They kicked my ass out the door and then things got *worse*!" Serena pouted, "Come on, Zoe, you remember how good it felt to put that parking meter through my brother's shoulder? Remember how good it feels to kick some ass? There's a neon-painted bitch in there with your name on her; she makes the whole dyed-hair thing look like a course at clown college!"

Zoey sighed, "Okay. Okay! What's the address again?"

Serena frowned, "The address? It's the only damn office building downtown that's been renovated in less than a week! You can't get a damn wheelchair ramp built fucking *anywhere* around here, but they get this place rebuilt in—"

"Zane? You alright?" Zoey frowned.

"That office building..." Zane bit his lip.

"What about it?"

"I... I think I remember being there," Zane frowned.

"Well, Axle *did* end up misplacing a lot of money on their roof shortly after you'd been put in his body," Serena offered.

"No. Not *on* or *near*. I was *in* that building! I'm not sure how, but I remember..." Zane shook his head.

"Zane?" Serena frowned, "Do you know where you went after that Kristine bitch pulled your aura out of your body?"

"Kristine..." His eyes suddenly went wide and Serena frowned as his body began to shake as his anger began to snake through him.

"Zane! What is it? What's wrong?" Serena placed her hand on his shoulder.

"Kristine!" Zane growled, "That night when Kristine came to attack you..." He shook his head, "When she attacked and I was struck. My aura... It was her! I was stuck with her!" He looked at Serena, "Just like how Devon was bound to your aura! And she was *constantly* in that building with... with somebody else. Some partner in building that place…"

"Which means she's the one that put you inside Axle!" Serena narrowed her eyes. "That fucking bitch! Why in the fuck would The Council give *her* permission to start a clan?"

Isaac frowned, "Did you ever hear that straight from anyone in The Council? Or was it just word-of-mouth? If they're privately bankrolled and making claims to anybody of power that they're acting as an extension of *us* because of our proximity, then they don't really need to answer to *anybody* as long as nobody figures out their angle."

"Son of a bitch!" Serena growled, "That fucking cunt is going down!"

"I'm with you!" Zoey announced.

"Same here!" Isaac smirked.

"You may need some extra magic and muscle in there!" Nikki stepped out with Raith at her side.

"Serena…" Zoey frowned, biting her lip as she watched the scene as well, "We need to make a plan."

"You know what I'm planning already, Zoey." Serena smirked, "We go in there and take those fuckers down!"

"We attack tomorrow at dusk!"

"Dusk, huh?" Zane smirked, "sounds like a good time to me!"

CHAPTER TWENTY-ONE
BATTLEFIELD

THE PARTING SUN'S RAYS HAD FINALLY past the horizon, leaving a smoky red sky as the hint of the moon hid behind the painted clouds. The skies scarlet hues had Serena ready for their attack.

It was time...

Time to end Kristine.

Time to put the past to rest.

As they filed into their cars, Serena hopped on her motorcycle and grinned as she revved the engine, signaling to the others before she started off, the others not far behind.

Clackity clack clack clackityclack clack clack clack clackity.
Tiffany sighed, already bored and feeling herself lulled by the rhythm of her nails working the keyboard as another day of work went by. The job had become a total drag since the bosses had come down on her for letting the Vailean girl get the drop on her so many times. To make matters worse, most of the security guards had quit after they'd seen what had happened to their friends, and, with the whole mess being blamed on *her*, Tiffany had been forced to actually start keeping up with her work.

Which would have been so much easier if that bitch hadn't broken her fingers!

Just fifteen minutes.

Just fifteen short minutes until the end of shift.

Then she could just go home and...

Seeing a flood of light fill the front window, she lifted her head to get a better view of what was beyond the recently-fixed door.

Her eyes went wide.

Fifteen minutes seemed so far away suddenly...

Serena steered the motorcycle off the street and popped a wheelie before the first of the steps that led up to the office building's front door. Throwing her aura in a makeshift slingshot, she pulled the bike's wheels from the staircase and launched her and the bike at the front door.

"Knock knock, assholes!"

Wrapping herself in an auric shield, Serena crashed the bike through the glass—the others in the Hummer following suit just behind her—and sent a hailstorm of broken glass spraying out across the interior of the lobby

Letting her motorcycle fall to the floor, Serena pulled drew the katana that was sheathed at her side. Spotting the source of so many previous bad moods, she jumped into overdrive and appeared in front of the neon-painted nuisance with the tip of the blade pressed to her throat.

"You crazy fucking bitch!" The secretary sneered, "Do you, like, *know* what The Council's going to do to you when they find out abou—"

"Tiffany, right?" Serena smirked and nodded, "Yea. See: while you were flapping your gums just now, I decided to take a swim in your head. Now, for starters: yuck; you are a whole new breed of worthless trash. But, more importantly, I just saw *everything* in your head about this place." She made a note of giving a slight drag with the sword across the side of her neck, earning a small trickle of blood. "Now I don't even want to hear your voice, so I'll make you a deal: if you nod your head and agree that what I saw in your mind is true—that this entire 'clan' thing is a hoax and that you're a worthless patsy who has never even *seen* the leaders or knows their names; just a bunch of emails from upstairs telling you to send *anybody* who comes in right back out again—and I'll forgive all of it and *not* execute you for treason."

The secretary nodded.

"Good," Serena smiled, lowering the sword. "Now there's just the matter of that eleven year old boy you kidnapped a month and a half ago to use as your own personal feeder. That's a criminal offense"—Serena smirked—"punishable by, like, the death penalty!"

"No, wait! Plea—"

Serena let out a deep sigh of relief as the neon-painted head hit the floor.

Zane stepped up behind her, looking down at it. "Yeesh!"

Serena nodded, "You're telling me."

The others gathered around Serena and braced themselves as the pounding sound of footsteps grew louder from beyond the door to the hallway ahead of them.

"Here we go!"

"About time!" Zane smirked, flexing his fists. "I've been aching for a good fight!"

A wave of mythos in uniform burst from the doors and started towards them, the first three soon hitting the floor without their heads as Serena made a wide pass with her sword. As the fourth ducked under the attack, the next countered with their own blade; forcing Serena's katana away from the other guards as they began to flood the room.

"Zoey," Serena glanced back, "I think the boys have had enough privacy."

An unnerving giggle issued from the blue-haired auric then and the auric veil that had been hiding Isaac and Raith—already waiting in their therion forms—lifted and revealed the two hulking creatures standing on either side of the doors. The first few guards made muffled sounds from under their helmets as they tried to flee, only to find that their feet were suddenly locked to the floor.

Courtesy of a stealthy spell from Nikki, who'd melted the soles of the boots before flash-cooling them to the linoleum.

Casting out her aura and warping the blade of the distracted guard who'd countered her, Serena drove a fist into his gut. As he keeled over, Serena met the face-plate of his helmet with her knee—shattering the fiberglass shielding in his face—and brought the butt of her sword's handle down on the exposed nape of his neck.

Zoey and Isaac had split to the left and were taking on a group of guards that had flocked around the back to try to close in on the group. Zoey's aura whipped out—going in a wide arc from one end of the room to the other—and wrapped around the guards as she ducked and dipped under their attacks. When the bulk of their attackers were secured in her invisible grip, Isaac began to go to work. There was no need for weapons; the therion only needed half-a-minute and the assets nature had granted him.

Serena frowned as she heard more footsteps approaching on the right and she swung around right Nikki and Raith rushed forward to help.

"I got them!" Nikki called out as she pulled out her sais—the metal shimmering with the added magic of her magical tattoos—and began to charge through the crowd; a violent whirlwind of enchanted metal and well-cast spells leaving a trail of bodies as she passed.

Raith, satisfied that his work in the lobby was finished, dropped to all fours and loped after Nikki before finally joining her at her side; rising to his complete height and making a note of bringing a massive fist down on the head of the nearest guard; forcing his skull and most of his helmet through the top of his chest.

"Looks like they got this, babes. You ready to head up?" Zane smirked.

"I've been ready!" Serena grinned.

The two rushed into the elevators and Serena sighed, readying herself for what was to come. Adrenaline rushed through her veins, flooding her system with just the right sort of fuel. She frowned, trying to catch her breath and slow the growing sense of dread. So much had happened—so much to warrant this kill—and yet, she was suddenly afraid.

"Serena...you okay?" Zane frowned, pressing his hand to her shoulder.

"I'll be fine," she smiled. "Just pre-show jitters."

The elevator doors creaked open and Serena's eyes widened as a caged-off region in the room was suddenly opened by several guards brandishing cattle prods, which they used to herd four ykalis towards them.

"I *knew* she was weaponizing the ykalis!" Serena glared.

"Are you fucking serious? They're keeping these things as *pets*?" Zane growled.

Serena looked over at Zane as he gave her a reassuring smile and Serena felt her anxieties ease instantly.

"Let's make this fast!" Zane growled out as he rushed forward, drawing a pair of pistols and beginning to fire at the charging monsters.

Serena grinned, pausing to appreciate her man work before she rushed in to join him, wielding her auric "bow" and filling the room with bright purple "arrows". Between Zane's and Serena's combined efforts, the four ykali had just below a minute of time to regret their existence before bits and pieces of themselves began to fall from their bodies.

Two corpses filled with bullets and the aurically divided bits of the other two.

And, at the end of the stretch of carnage, two sangsuigan guards who'd died with their buzzing cattle prods still firmly held in their hands.

Starting for the staircase at the end of the room, the two began working their way up the building, using the narrow and Serena's auric "view" of what was coming to their advantage. As they continued ever higher, more and more pieces of more and more guards began to rain down in their wake.

Until they finally reached a floor with a familiar auric signature waiting on the other side.

Welcome back, Serena! Kristine's psychic voice called out and Serena growled, tearing the door off the hinges with her aura.

Stay here, she paused to send a private message to Zane and mask his aura from detection. *She probably doesn't know that you're back, let alone back in your own body. We can use that. Just wait...*

Stepping through the door, Serena spotted her target and bared her fangs as she squared off against Kristine.

"I was wondering how long it would take you to show up here."

CHAPTER TWENTY-TWO
LESSON LEARNED

"*YOU!*" SERENA CRIED OUT AS she rushed forward towards Kristine.

Kristine smirked and coiled her pale-green aura around Serena's body as she threw her against the wall.

"You've always been so rash, Serena," she smirked, stepping forward slowly. "I didn't have to worry about whether or not all this would work out; I just had to trust that, if it didn't, you'd be predictable enough to do *exactly* what you've done. That's the problem with always letting your emotions lead you."

"Shut up!" Serena glared, standing up and shaking debris off her as she stepped forward. "Don't act like you know me! You've been a thorn in my side since you killed Devon, but you've *never* been able to figure out *why* you're so obsessed with coming back!

You want to play the 'stupid emotional twat' game? Try looking at yourself for a change!"

"Ah, yes. Poor Devon" Kristine glared, "The man you *claimed* to love so much until Zane came into the picture."

"I did love Devon!" Serena growled and began to throw her aura out in jagged bursts, "I could *never* have been driven to kill him for *any* reason! *You*, you stupid jealous bitch, killed him because you were pissy that he hadn't chosen you! You're nothing but a spoiled little brat throwing a tantrum because her puppy liked somebody else more!"

Kristine growled, "Shut up! It was *your* new *psychotic* pet that finally destroyed Devon!" She glared, dodging and blocking the auric spikes and shook her head, "You are going to have to be better than *that*!"

Kristine lunged then and slammed her fist in Serena's stomach, using her aura to propel the punch and grinned at Serena's pained expression. Serena frowned, gasping as blood spilled from her lips and frowned.

She couldn't lose!

Not now!

Not ever!

Not when everything was suddenly so clear.

"Zane can't be blamed for taking Devon from this world," Serena hissed, spitting a wad of blood in Kristine's face. "It was *your* carelessness—your fucking jealousy making you every bit the stupid bitch you've allowed yourself to become—that did that." Kristine glared and tried to open her mouth to speak, but her auric shields were fractured—weakened by her emotions—and Serena wormed her aura into her mind and locked her jaw in a psychic bind. "No, Kristine. You've wasted your voice enough for one lifetime," Serena started towards her letting her aura section off into three tendrils—two forming miniature crossbows in each hand while the third whipped back-and-forth from her chest—and started to march towards her. "And even after *you* fucked up and killed the man you claimed to love, he came back to *me*! You're a special breed of loser, Kristine; the kind that would *kill* the puppy for playing with the neighbor boy, and then throw a tantrum when the puppy's ghost didn't bark outside her window." Serena scoffed, "He didn't even care enough about you to *haunt* you!"

"SHUT UP!" Kristine glared, hurling her aura out at Serena

only to have the whipping tendril deflect it.

Serena shook her head, "Wait, it gets better: because Zane—the one you *blame* for 'taking Devon away' despite *your* murdering him without *any* guarantee that he'd come back—only reacted to Devon's fractured personality; a personality that'd still be whole if not for you. And when Devon's mind was too far gone to make the right decisions, it got him the peace he should have been allowed in the first place." She narrowed her eyes at her, "The difference between you and me isn't that I'm a stupid bitch and you're not, the difference is that *you're* a stupid bitch who can't own up to it and admit that sometimes the fault is just your own!"

She raised the two auric crossbows and took aim.

"And now, you boring, repugnant cocksucker, you have to die!"

Suddenly Devon was standing in front of her.

"D-Devon?" Serena whispered, "It... It can't be..."

"It's me, Serena..." He stepped forward and placed his hand on her cheek.

"No, Kristine," Serena leveled one of the auric crossbows to Devon's chest. "If you'd been listening, you'd know that I've made peace with the fact that Devon's gone, and there's nothing that—"

"Serena?" Zane stepped out from behind Kristine, "You have to stop thi—"

Serena rolled her eyes. "Oh, come on, you stupid bitch! You're not even—Zane! Will you please come out and show Kristine what a stupid bitch she is?"

Zane's aura spiked from the staircase where she'd left him and he poked his head out, "Huh? Do you need help or something?"

Kristine's eyes widened.

Serena smirked, "No, that was enough. Thanks, babes."

"Uh... Yea. No problem," Zane nodded.

Serena turned back, shooting two "bolts" from each of the auric crossbows—two through the fake-Devon and into Kristine's right shoulder and hip, one through the fake-Zane and into Kristine's left thigh, and the last in Kristine's chest—and walked through the Devon illusion as it faded. Slumped against the floor, Serena watched as Kristine struggled against the auric binds that pinned her against the wall.

"Probably should've mentioned that Zane's back, and in his own body, no less." Serena shrugged, "Thought that Axle trick was pretty clever, huh?" Serena's auric crossbows faded from her hands, leaving only the purple tendril that extended from her chest, "Now, as I was saying: it's time to die."

"Y-you're for-getting... my grea-greatest fault," Kristine whimpered.

Serena sighed, "Well, since you're probably going to bleed out soon you might as well tell me."

Kristine chuckled against the pain, "If... I can't win... I won't let... anybody... win..."

Turning her aura inward on herself, Kristine's life-force snuffed itself and triggered an auric burst, consuming Serena in the blast.

"She still hasn't woken up?" Zane growled, driving his fist repeatedly into the empty gurney neighboring Serena's body. "You said her aura's active; you said that she was going to pull out of it! It's been *eight* goddam hours! Why hasn't she woken up yet?"

Zoey bit her lip, "I... I can't answer that, Zane. Nobody can. I've been feeding *twice* the standard energy doses into her and I've got her on a synthetic blood drip that's *four times* the concentration of what we used to wake you up when you were in Axle's body. Biologically, she *should* be bouncing around like a damn a hummingbird, but there has been *a lot* of stress and pain on her ever since you were taken," she sighed. "I think that she's exhausted, Zane; I think that her mind is taking a vacation to recuperate from all the sleepless, lonely nights and all the fear that she'd never get to see you again." Putting the files aside and wrapping her arms around her friend, she used the contact with her left hand to drain some of his anxiety. "The most you can do right now is just be there for her."

Zane sighed and nodded, looking back at Serena and smiling. "Well, at least we all made it out of there, right?"

Zoey chuckled, "You *know* she's going to taunt me about being right when she wakes up, right?"

"Can't really blame her," Zane smirked, "She was right about *everything*!"

"Can you do me a favor and *not* feed her that gloating right for at least a day?"

"Only if you do me a favor," Zane smirked.

Zoey groaned, "What?"

"I am *dying* to get a Slushie and a cheap, nasty gas station hot dog in my belly, and I'm sure Serena would love to have a Snickers and one of those magazines she's always reading. Do you think you could drive me to the city and front me the cash to grab the goods?"

Zoey frowned, "Why can't you drive and buy your own garbage?"

"Because then it wouldn't be a favor," Zane chuckled.

"I guess that makes sense… sort of," Zoey nodded. "Alright, fine."

Zane frowned and looked over. "Why are we keeping that *thing* in here?"

Zoey looked over at the ykali body that was still being infused with the *Maledictus* curse and frowned, "Because that's a corpse…?" She frowned, "and we're in the medical center. Would you rather we kept it in the cafeteria?"

Zane frowned at the creature and shrugged, "I guess I just don't like the idea that it could suddenly wake up."

"Doubt it. It's not that it's not going to wake up *eventually*, but *that's* been out without *any* sign of life—no pulse, no brain activity, and barely any measureable auric activity—for *days*, where Serena's breathing and dreaming no differently than if she was just napping. Between the two of them, I'm willing to bet that Serena's going to be the first to open her eyes."

Zane frowned, glancing back at Serena. "You promise?"

"STOP THE CAR!" Zane cried, barely letting Zoey complete the stop before he was grabbing at the door handle and trying to get out of the car.

"What is it?" Zoey asked, looking in her mirrors, frantic to know if she'd done something wrong, "Did I hit something?"

Zane shook his head—his eyes wide and unblinking as he

stepped from the car and stared down the sidewalk. Unable to bear the tension and suspense, Zoey threw the car into park and stepped out, as well. Stepping over to stare in the direction of Zane's unseen obsession, Zoey frowned at the simple and common sight of people walking around the city streets.

"Zane...?" Zoey frowned, looking up at her friend, "You're scaring me. What are you looking for?"

"I..." Zane shook his head and sighed, rubbing the back of his neck. "I thought I saw somebody I used to know. Sorry about that."

Zoey shrugged and started back towards the car. "Happens to the best of us, I suppose."

Getting back to the clan, Zane started back towards the medical center, daring to flip through a few of the magazines he'd picked up for Serena.

"'Ten ways to please your man with just your toes'? What the fuck is wrong with this women? Serena, I swear to god, if you *ever* try *any* of these things on me—well, I guess number seven looks alright... hmm—but yea, if you—"

The magazines clattered to the floor along with the extra-large Slushie and Zane's half-eaten hotdog.

The room was in shambles.

Half of the equipment was ripped from the walls and in pieces; the other half had been fortunate enough to be out of commission on the other side of the room. Supplies and materials were strewn about like confetti, and the room was littered with ykali scales.

And Serena's gurney was empty...

With nothing but a tuft of platinum-blonde hair to testify to the owner's abduction...

To be concluded in Scarlet Dusk
By Megan J. Parker

Preview to Original Sin (A Crimson Shadow Novella)
Megan J. Parker
(Available Now)

Chapter One
~Emily~

THE CLOUDS SHIFTED IN THE STARLIT SKY and allowed for the full moon to illuminate the city in its silvery glow as I stepped out from the lifeless luminescence of the hospital. As I started out, I spotted three of the doctors standing by the entranceway as they gave me *that* look and I bit my lip at their flirting stares. It wasn't that they or any of the other doctors who gave me *that* look weren't good looking, and it certainly wasn't that I was uninterested in finding love…

It just didn't feel right with them.

There just wasn't that—

"Hey, Emily," Phil, one of the more daring doctors on our staff, shot his trademark smirk my way, "Did you want to join us at the bar tonight?"

"Oh! Thanks for the offer, but I really should get home tonight. I'm already feeling lagged," I forced a soft smile as I recited the same excuse I did every night after work.

"Aw! One of these days, Emily," he chided me, "One of these days we're gonna wear you down."

I chuckled and quickly excused myself, making my way through the parking lot and into the city lights. With the hushed murmurs of my admirers too distant to hear, I let out a heavy breath and shook my head at myself.

I didn't understand it, really. I spent most of my free time reading romance novels and daydreaming about finding my own personal Prince Charming, and yet, whenever the reality of an interested suitor sprung up, I couldn't bring myself to accept them; couldn't even give them a chance. I sighed again. Maybe it was time to put down the books—to abandon the fantasies and fiction—and just settle...

I felt myself shudder at the thought of lowering my more-than-likely outlandish standards and slipped away from the bustling crowd and into an alleyway to catch my breath. As my own labored breathing and thundering heartbeat settled, I picked up on another set of heavy breaths—loud and pained—and, fighting my growing nerves, looked deeper into the darkness of the alley to see the source.

"Oh my—" My heartbeat started up again and I instinctively started forward. Ahead of me, a large-framed man was crouched and clutching a blood-drenched hand over his stomach. "Sir! Are you alright? Were you injured? It's okay, I'm a—"

My words caught in my throat as the man lifted his head at the sound of my voice, wincing at his own movement and letting out a hissed breath at the pain. I gasped, feeling the chill of the opposite wall against my back.

Had I even moved?

I shook my head; trying to remember stepping back but drawing a blank.

"I-I'm fine," his voice cracked and he coughed; spitting blood on the alley floor. "Just... just go!"

Taking a deep breath, I forced myself to step forward again

and knelt beside him to check his wounds. Though whatever injury he had was hidden, I could tell that the blood was recent and I moved to pry his hands away to better inspect the damage. Still keeping one hand on his abdomen, he snatched me by the wrist and looked up at me.

"Ple-please," his voice was suddenly desperate, "You... you need to go. Now!"

"I..." My breath hitched in my chest as our gazes collided, his dark hazel eyes peering deep into me.

I could get lost in those eyes.

I shook my head, trying to clear my thoughts. "I can't do that, sir. I'm a nurse; I've taken an oath to help the injured!"

I tried not to think about the lie I was telling as I spoke the words. I wasn't exactly *required* to help anyone outside of office and, quite frankly, I'd ignored several situations in the past when I'd stumbled across the aftermath of a drunken brawl or some other minor incident that I felt was too dangerous to get involved in.

But this situation had "danger" written all over it!

So why was I doing this?

Why did I stop for him?

"You don't need to lie," he let out a small laugh, "I'll be alright soon. Thank you, Emily."

I frowned at that.

Had I told him my...

I shook my head again. "W-well, maybe I just want to help you. And, trust me, when I decide to do something, I don't stop until I do it!"

The man stifled a chuckle, "That stubbornness is going to get you into trouble."

My eyes widened as his words echoed in my mother's voice in the back of my head. She'd always said that my stubbornness was going to get—

"A-Alright..." He moved from his slouched position, "If you insist." He groaned in pain as he straightened himself and lifted his blood-stained shirt. I fought the heat that threatened to crawl up my face his toned abdomen and broad chest was revealed to me.

Realizing that I was still staring, I moved to reach into my handbag for my flashlight. Though the rays of the moon were enough to illuminate his features, the depth and darkness of the alley made it hard to do the job I'd set my mind on doing.

"Okay. I'm going to need you to stay still and relax as best as you can."

"Alright. If you say so…" He flashed me a grin of perfect teeth and I desperately fought the urge to swoon. Then, as if he could tell the effect he was having, he added, "Nurse Emily."

His tone…

It was as if the pain was…

I ignored my wandering thoughts as I aimed the beam of light at his torso. I gasped as I got a clear view of the source of all the blood. He'd been shot! Moving around him, I searched his back for an exit-wound. If the bullet was still inside…

"You really should see a doctor. I can't treat a gunshot wound. I don't have the supplies, and you need to file a report with the po—"

"I said I'd be fine," his smirk forced another wave of warmth to my cheeks.

"'Fine'? How can you say that?" My emotions flared at his casualness to the situation, "How can you be so calm about this? You've been shot! And… and I think the bullet is still—" I shook my head, "Dammit! You're going to bleed to death if you don't—"

I gasped as he lifted his left hand and placed it on my hand; a sudden wave of ease and calm sweeping over me.

"—If… if you don't…" I stammered, trying to remember what I'd been thinking. I'd been angry, hadn't I? All of a sudden I couldn't remember…

This man…

I looked down at his hand on mine and felt another wave of warmth and calm. I'd never felt so relaxed, certainly not around strangers in alleys with bullet wounds. With him, however—with this eerily calm man—I felt my entire body ease and turned my hand into his palm, lacing my fingers with his and drawing on the warmth he was providing.

"You have beautiful hair, Emily," he smirked. "I've always had a thing for redheads. If it weren't for—well, you know"—he lifted his still blood-covered hand—"I might be compelled to touch it."

Despite the reminder of his injuries, my calmness held. "R-really? I always hated my hair. The curls are so unmanageable."

"Ah, but sometimes the most untamable things can be the most beautiful of all," he smirked.

"That...that was *really* cheesy," I blushed at how simple it was to talk to him given the circumstances.

"Aw man! Add my ego to the list of injuries. That sort of line usually works on the girls," he chuckled. "You're a rare breed, Emily."

I lifted my eyes back to his face and blushed, the wind had swept his messy black hair out of his face and I was able to see him fully. He was so handsome.

Too handsome!

I frowned. I was so certain that I'd never... "How do you know my name?" I forced myself to ask, shaking the numbing calmness. "I... I never told you... Who are you?"

It felt like I'd just taken a shot of morphine!

"My name's Joseph—Joseph Stryker—and I know you didn't tell me your name," he shrugged, smirking at my obvious appraisal of his features, and licked his lips, "I just have my ways."

"Then... then how?" I frowned, the uneasiness sweeping back into me as his hand left mine and I watched as he stood up and started to pull his shirt back on. "W-wait," I struggled to follow, suddenly feeling dizzy, "How did you know my name?"

Joseph smiled at me and shook his head, "No more questions, Emily. I've already said too much."

I gaped as he lifted my right hand and placed a kiss against my palm and I bit my lip as a shiver made its way up my spine.

Finally, drawing his lips away from my hand, he gently worked my fingers closed. "Hold on to that for me, Emily," he took a deep breath and stretched, showing no sign of his injuries. "Thanks again. I will remember the help you gave me today and find a way to repay you."

"N-no problem. Really. You don't have to repay me... I-I mean, I probably won't even see you again anyway."

"Maybe; maybe not," he shrugged, "Either way, just try not to remember me. I probably shouldn't have..." he frowned and shook his head. "Just... just don't worry about me." He offered me one last blush-inducing smirk, "Besides, I couldn't compete with Doctor Phil."

With that he turned away and stepped out of the alley.

Staring after him, I felt the last of the numbness on my mind faded away. Finally, I growled with the realization that he had just tricked me; used some quick words and an intoxicating gaze to avoid my question. Refusing to be his fool, I rushed out of the alleyway to track him down, only to find that he had already disappeared into the crowd.

Who was that man?

And how did he know my name?

Sighing, I turned towards my street and headed off to my apartment. It would be better not to see Joseph Stryker again, I told myself. Men like that was disastrous to women. It was men like that that made the stories in those damn romance novels seem so within reach. As I made my way to my apartment, I unlocked the door and headed inside.

"Aries! Where's my handsome man?" I called out as I switched on the light. A soft mewl sounded from my room before the mischievous black cat trotted towards me and rubbed against my ankle. "Aw! Did you miss me?" I smiled and kneeled down to pet him before starting towards the kitchen, "Come on. I bet you're just as hungry as I am."

Plopping a TV dinner into the microwave, I grumbled at the realization that it was already 1am and I had to be back at the hospital in only six short hours.

Where had the night gone?

Had I *really* been in the alley *that* long?

I ate my dinner in a slow haze, each bite bringing with it less and less flavor and more and more questions. It wasn't until my fork had found an empty plate that I realized I'd actually eaten anything, and I decided that what I wanted—what I truly needed—was a shower.

As I made my way to the bathroom and began to slip out of my clothes my thoughts returned to Joseph. Remembering him—his face and his body and his drug-like touch—brought the warmth back and I shivered as it began to spread through my stomach. I lingered, envisioning his toned arms encircling my waist and pulling me against that perfect torso as he…

I shook my head, fighting past the erotic fantasy, and I forced myself to step into the tub and draw the shower curtain. Grabbing the soap, I began my routine as I let my mind wander again. Instinctively, my hand drifted past my stomach and I gasped; every part of me felt electrified. I growled at myself and shook my head; I had *never* felt this way before. How could I let a stranger affect me this much? He was just a—

The sound of my phone ringing quickly cooled me down and I wrapped a towel around me as I hurried see who could be calling me at this hour.

"Hello?"

"Emily! Did I wake you?" I bit my lip, hearing Doctor Thane's voice.

"No, I just got home. Is something wrong?" I asked, pretending to sound surprised even though I already knew what he was calling about. Though my degree should have spoken for itself, I was certain that he'd only hired me in the hopes of motivating a relationship. Ever since the first time I'd turned him down, he'd been relentless in his pursuit and I was worried that sooner or later I would be forced into saying "yes" just to keep my job.

"Just got home? But your shift ended almost an hour ago!" I could hear the seething jealousy growing in his voice and I fought the urge to hang up on him.

"I... uh, yea," I rubbed the back of my neck and struggled to hide my own shock from my voice. An hour? How was that even possible?

"Emily?"

"Yea—sorry—I'm here. I just had some grocery shopping I needed to do. I guess I lost track of time," I answered, though I was certain it wasn't his place to need an answer. I suddenly felt exposed being in just the towel even though I was only on the phone with him.

"Oh, I see. Well, I was calling to see if you had an answer to my proposal yet?"

I cupped my hand on the receiver and groaned, glaring at the phone as though my cold stare might freeze him on the other end. A "proposal" he called it; like dating me was a business endeavor!

"I have and, Michael, I'm afraid that—"

"There's no rush, Emily. Give it some more thought. I'm sorry about calling you this late, I'm sure you are barely of the mind to give me an answer. I will talk to you later. Good night."

"Barely of the—Hey! Wai—" I frowned, as the receiver went dead and I slammed the phone down.

The nerve of some people! I growled as I headed back to the shower and let myself fall back into the water's warm embrace.

Hopefully, tomorrow would be a better day.

Preview to Crimson Shadow: Forbidden Dance (Book 3) Nathan Squiers (Available Now)

Chapter Twenty:
Defense

Journal entry: December 15th

ESTELLA,

After some thought and a severe, supernatural ass-kicking, I've decided that what I did was justified. I understand that you're hesitant to accept what you are now, but you need to come to grips with it before it gets you killed.

There's some bad, dangerous humans (if they can be called that anymore) out there killing lots of innocent mythos, and I need to make sure that you don't become one of their victims.

Now that I have seen your aura and I know what I'm looking for, I WILL find you, and I will bring you back with me.

Nothing will stop me from saving you and showing you how sorry I am for what happened and how much I love you!

Xander

Xander closed the notebook and set down the pen. He wasn't sure why he'd felt compelled to write that one last letter before going out to make things right, but after months and months of writing letters to Estella that he was positive would never be read it just seemed like the right thing to do.

Timothy, who had patiently sat nearby with a toy gun that Xander had bought him and exterminating imaginary enemies, glanced up at him with eager eyes as his mentor rose to his feet; excited to know what was in store for him. Xander smiled at his apprentice and ruffled his hair before patting his shoulder.

"I want you to train with Zeek again tonight."

Timothy frowned, "You're leaving again?"

Xander nodded, "It's important; very important. But I promise that when I get back everything will be alright."

"What about the hunters?" Timothy's voice cracked.

"Don't worry about them," Xander smirked, "You're already tough enough to take both of them on one-handed."

Timothy laughed nervously, "I don't know…"

Xander shrugged, "Maybe you're right. But soon," his smile widened. "You're doing really well."

Timothy blushed at the compliment, but quickly looked away and frowned, "What if they come tonight while you're gone?"

"They won't."

"But what if they do?" The little vampire demanded.

Xander frowned, "Then I want you to run—run faster than you've ever run before—and find the best hiding place you can; let the others fight."

"But if they fight then they'll die!" Timothy's eyes were beginning to water.

"They may," Xander saw no reason to lie, not about this, "But they'd all proudly die to make sure you lived, so you can't let them down. Understand?"

Timothy wiped his eyes and nodded.

"Good," Xander stepped out of the tent, "I won't be long."

Zeek was already waiting outside for them as they emerged. Timothy smiled at the sight and stepped from Xander's side to join the anapriek, and Xander couldn't help but smile at the little vampire's strength and eagerness.

Xander silently promised himself that he wouldn't let anything happen to him.

"Be sure to kick his ass," Xander chuckled.

Zeek glared at him but said nothing in protest as he took Timothy's hand and turned away, leading him off.

Estella was close—at least she hoped she was. She'd been walking for several hours now, her trek into the forest starting in the late afternoon, when the sun was still hanging in the sky. She'd been up all day anyway, wandering and thinking life-changing thoughts.

Her mind was still a jumbled mess that she was slowly working to organize when she first heard the growling. Like an audible bear-trap, it picked up as her foot touched down on the frost-bitten forest floor; ensnaring her in a fearful tremor. Her first instinct was to step back away, hoping that reversing the step she'd taken would appease the creature.

It didn't.

Instead it grew louder as whatever was making the sound came closer.

Xander had told her about therions. The description had been slightly biased at the time, the explanation coming shortly after he'd almost been killed by one of the creatures, but somehow it still came out sounding strangely beautiful. Unlike the legends of werewolves, therions didn't simply come in the one shape. Like humans, there were all different sizes and shapes to them.

As Estella stood there, watching the creature charge at her now, however, it wasn't as easily labeled as Xander had made it sound. Large, broad shoulders like a gorilla pumped as it loped forward, its body the color of burnt toast and speckled with spots like a leopard. A large, brownish-red mane of hair flurried about its head as it came, and the jaws that snapped were broad, the muzzle jutting out like a bear's.

It was massive.

And it was angry.

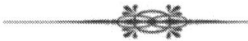

Xander was nearby when he first heard the snarls; unmistakably Inarin's. The therion was probably one of the biggest he'd ever seen, and by far one of the pack's most loyal members. Xander had seen him fight only once several months earlier when they all tried to hunt down and kill Lenix. Though they'd failed, most of his mind-controlled army had been destroyed, and Inarin had more brought down more than his share.

But what had him so worked up now?

Had the warrior from the other night come back to try and convince him once again to join their efforts against the hunters?

Whatever it was, it was about to get ripped apart.

And then Xander sensed it.

The familiar auric signature…

Estella!

He was in overdrive and rocketing in the direction of the sounds before he'd fully registered what he was doing. Her aura, a darker shade of orange than it had been before, shone in the distance like a beacon. He pushed himself to go faster than he'd ever moved before. Inarin's golden-brown aura was nearly on top of Estella's own! Though time was practically frozen for the world around him he knew it wouldn't be long before…

NO!

He couldn't allow it!

He knew that the moment he jumped off the ground he'd be thrown back into normal time, and he fought to gain enough momentum to combat the unforgiving force of nature.

He had to time it perfectly!

When he was practically right under his pack-mate he threw himself upward with every bit of strength and speed he had. Shifting Inarin's course would not be simple. As he crashed into the therion's massive form he saw the world around him suddenly spring back to life around him the two slammed into ground with enough force to tear the earth beneath them.

Xander was the first to his feet, breathing heavily and making sure he was between his snarling packmate and Estella. Inarin pulled himself up, standing at his full height as his lips peeled back and displayed his teeth. Xander countered with an angry hiss, baring his own fangs and flaring his aura so that the forest pushed and swayed away from him and the broken ground cratered even further beneath his feet.

He *would not* let anything take Estella away!

Not again!

And if that meant killing Inarin—killing a razor-sharp, nine-foot monster—then so be it!

"Xander…" Estella gasped.

Her voice was all the proof Xander needed to know she was

still alright, "Stay behind me."

Inarin roared, once again announcing his disapproval in the only audible way his bestial form would allow. Xander didn't need words or his psychic abilities to know what he was thinking, though. Estella was another trespasser among many; yet another outsider. This was the third time that their territory had been made infringed upon, and the majority of the pack had grown bloodthirsty after the first night when Zeek and the others had shown up.

This one last visitor had been the last straw, and Inarin was eager to vent his pent-up rage by spilling blood.

But it wouldn't be Estella's.

Not if Xander had anything to say about it.

Xander pointed back at Estella, never taking his scorching gaze off of the therion, "She lives," he growled, "She *LIVES*! You can have anybody else but her. Go into the city and rip apart all the humans it takes to calm your ass—put yourself on The Council's list of rogues to be executed—but you *will not* hurt her!" He hissed and took another step towards him, kicking up his aura once again, "Or I *will* kill you!"

The therion glanced over his shoulder at the trespasser, roaring and pounding his chest.

"You don't want it to happen this way," Xander assured him, already clenching his fists.

Inarin didn't listen.

He charged—running on all fours as he usually did when prepared for battle—before throwing himself into the air, ready to use his bulk to crush Xander in an attempt to get past him and to Estella. Seeing this intention—both reading his mind and having seen the tactic before—Xander leapt up to intercept the therion and brought his knee up, driving it into the underside of his comrade's snapping jaw hard enough to send the therion reeling backwards.

As Inarin crashed to the ground, Xander threw out his aura and held himself in midair for a moment before floating down, softening the landing for himself and his now-sore knee. Inarin was up in a flash, grabbing a young sapling and ripping it from the ground—its tortured roots snapping and raining clumps of soil—and brandishing it like a baseball bat. Xander bared his fangs again. The tree was swung with tremendous force, its branches whistling as they cut through the air. Just before impact, Xander wrapped his aura around himself like a shell and Inarin's weapon splintered and shattered around him.

The sound was like thunder.

OSEHR! Xander sent out a telepathic message, *GET OVER HERE, NOW!*

Inarin was in the air again, coming down like a wrecking ball. Xander, relying on his instinct, executed a back handspring that landed him several feet away from the spot that he'd been occupying; the spot that Inarin then crashed down upon. Though there was no way to know for sure, Xander was positive that it would have been enough force to shatter even a vampire's bones.

This was no longer about getting past him.

Inarin's fury had taken over, and he saw Xander as an enemy now.

Enraged by Xander's agility and difficult time he was having in his attempts at breaking him, Inarin roared again and pounded the ground before he charged once again. Dodging this, Xander pivoted to keep his position between his packmate and Estella and wrapped the ballistic therion in his aura, lifting him off the ground and throwing him several yards away. He was up and storming back towards them in seconds.

"YOU CAN'T TAKE HER!" Xander roared, sending out an auric blast.

Unable to see the crimson energy wave, Inarin continued onward until it collided with him and tore him off his feet and sent him into a pine tree. His aura pulsed erratically, telling Xander that he was dazed, and as he slid down the tree and onto the ground he rolled to his knees and whined—a loud and angry whimper.

"Stay down," Xander muttered, more a wish than a command.

The therion stood and started to approach, his body swaying as he struggled to stay upright on clumsy legs. When he was close enough he pulled back his arm, ready to punch Xander in the face with a fist the size of a football.

Osehr caught the powerful arm in his hand and instantly stilled him.

"Stand down!" The therion leader's voice was hard and intimidating, his left arm bulging as he partially transformed.

Xander gaped, never knowing his friend had that kind of control.

Inarin's aura spiked once in surprise and just as quickly withdrew as his senses returned to him. Seeing the seriousness in the pack leader's eyes, he whimpered and looked back at Xander and Estella, issuing a soft growl, and dropped his arm before he began to transform back to his human form—still an intimidating creature, Xander thought—and glared.

"She is *not* one of us," he spat, "No outsiders! That was our rule!"

"I wasn't one of you either," Xander replied, backing up to join Estella at her side. "She stays!" He looked over at his long-lost lover and realized that she was blushing and turned back to Inarin and frowned. "Now will you go put some pants on?"

Inarin narrowed his eyes and looked to Osehr, who nodded.

"Do as he says," he calmly commanded, "Make yourself decent. And see to it that the others do the same." He gave Estella a warm smile, "We have a very special guest joining us."

This brought a smile to Estella's face; the familiar, warm smile that Xander remembered from when she was human.

He couldn't help but smile as well.

About the Author

Megan J. Parker lives in upstate New York in a small town that is no easier to spell than it is to pronounce. She lives with her adoring fiancé, Nathan Squiers, and her two devil kitties, Trent and Yuki (don't let their innocent looks deceive you, they are devious little cats). Normally, she can be found with her face plastered to her MacBook Pro either designing a new book cover or writing/plotting her latest story.

On her down time, she likes reading and watching comedy or romantic movies. Her passion for telling stories is portrayed in all her work and when there's a story to tell, you can be sure she'll tell it to its full extent. She now is a co-owner for the up and coming publishing company, Tiger Dynasty Publishing, and is hoping to continue to expand this company to great lengths.

COMING SOON
from Megan J. Parker & Tiger Dynasty Publishing:

SCARLET DUSK

He would do anything to get her back...

Zane's back... And pissed!

Even with certain burdens overcome, he is losing his mind to the anger and loss. Now on the trail of his biggest nightmare, Zane has to come to grips with his own strength. But when the past climbs back to the surface, he's forced to make a choice that could change everything. But with the screams of Serena echoing in his head, he must find a way to save the day.

* * * *

Serena has never been more terrified.

And as every dusk that falls she feels the threat of losing all hope growing within. The only courage she can find is her faith in Zane's arrival and the love they share. But, with the days growing longer and her screams growing stronger, she can't seem to call upon the strength that was always there.

* * * *

With the end drawing near, will the two be able to find the power to overcome their largest challenge yet?

Or will this new conflict be too strong for them...

SCARLET RISING

(Guest Authored by Nathan Squiers)

Gregori Vailean always prided himself as a "by-the-book" warrior to the mythos Council. As leader of the Clan of Vail and a role model to all the vampires he's taken in, there has never been any room for doubt in his black-and-white world of right and wrong within the world of non-humans.

But all of that changed when he botched a very important mission.

****

Mia Wilder had always taken to her last name with a sense of pride and obligation. Working as an undercover agent on order by The Council, she was hailed as one of the few who could take on even the most dangerous of jobs and come out of it unscathed. In her world of adventure and mystery, there's never been a time—or desire—for structure or stability.

But when the wildest case of her life goes awry, being untouchable is the last thing on her mind.

****

Now, with the worlds of order and chaos colliding, there's nothing to stop the scarlet from rising.

Made in the USA
Middletown, DE
22 June 2016